THUNDER THIGHS

LARSSON SIBLING SERIES
BOOK 1

EVIE MITCHELL

THUNDER THIGHS PUBLISHING

Editors: Nicole Wilson, Evermore Editing
http://www.evermoreediting.wixsite.com/info
Hot Tree Publishing
Proofreading: Ashley Lewis, Geeky Girl Author Services
Illustrator: Laras Putri

ACKNOWLEDGEMENT OF COUNTRY

I acknowledge the Traditional Custodians of the lands on which I write, the Ngunnawal people, and pay my respect to elders both past and present.

I acknowledge the continued and deep spiritual relationship of the Australian Aboriginal and Torres Strait Islander peoples' to this land, and their unique cultural and spiritual relationships to the land, waters and seas and their rich contribution to society.

Always was, always will be.

To my husband, thanks for adoring my thunder thighs. This piece of ridiculous fluff is for you.

CONTENT WARNING AND TERMINOLOGY

This book contains graphic and explicit descriptions of sex. The book includes references to overcoming body image struggles, and learning to love your own skin.

The main female character does refer to herself and others as fat and chubby She is body-positive and does so because she believes there is nothing wrong with loving the body you are in.

SPOILERS
A marine emergency occurs in the mid-part of the book, as well as a head injury. Injuries are referenced and described.
END SPOILERS

While all care has been taken to ensure representation is respectful and inclusive, my sensitivity readers and my personal experience is limited to our own knowledge and understanding. If there is anything in the book that raises concerns for you, please feel free to reach out to EvieMitchellAuthor@gmail.com.

THUNDER THIGHS

Ella

I'd always been told I had thunder thighs. Chunky, thick, beautiful—I embraced my curves, waiting for the right Thunder God to come along and rock my world. Then Gunnar Larsson strode his tall, blonde Viking butt through my bar doors. My thighs were awaiting his plunder.

Gunnar

Walking into Ella Bronze's bar was the best decision I'd made all year. Fuck, all decade. The gorgeous bombshell had curves for days— the kind that made me drool. There was no way this seductive siren was escaping. Looked like it was time to do what my ancestors did best— take what I wanted.

Warning: This over-the-top piece of fluff is inspired by big thighs, sexy Vikings, and a desire to have your pussy plundered. Get thee a Viking and settle in—this instalove story will blow you off course.

PROLOGUE

Ella

"...which brings me to the small town of Capricorn Cove. The Isle of Astipia, a small island kingdom that sits roughly halfway between the UK and North America, holds many hidden gems. But few as beautiful as this."

The camera panned out, showing a bird's eye view of the Cove.

"With its rugged coastline, pristine beaches, and quaint town—not to mention its proximity to the mountains and skiing in winter—the only thing this area lacks to attract a thriving tourist market is a decent place to eat."

The host of the travel show winked at the camera.

"But fear not, there's a local food truck called *The Bronze Horseman* that provides the best and freshest fish and chips I've ever eaten."

Anika hit freeze on her phone before shoving it in my face. "See!" she demanded, hopping up and down like a jackrabbit. "See?"

I leaned into our food van, attempting to avoid her flailing limbs. "That we're mentioned on an international travel show?"

"Yes! It's like I told you, Ella. There's a market for us." She twirled, her feet kicking up dirt in the gravel carpark. With almost aggressive excitement, she jabbed a finger at the abandoned building towering before us. "*This* is going to be our restaurant."

My lips quirked. "Oh, so you didn't drive me to an abandoned building in hopes of killing me for the insurance money."

My best friend shot me a disgruntled look. "Quit joking. This is our restaurant, Ella. This is The Bronze Horseman."

Located at the very end of the town's main street and a short stroll down from the marina, the rundown wreck sat on a gigantic lot that consisted of mostly trash and weeds. Once upon a time, it had held a hardware and garden store with generous outdoor areas and a parking lot. Now it seemed destined to become a breeding ground for tetanus.

I kicked a rusting beer can, listening as it rattled in the quiet. "This? Really?"

"Absolutely."

Decades ago, Capricorn Cove had been a thriving fishing town with a bustling port and plentiful tourists and businesses. But when the town's primary employer had decided to move their fishing production to one of the main islands, the town had been decimated overnight. Left with half-empty homes, a poorly maintained marina, and architecture in desperate need of a revamp. Our small town had long been struggling to rediscover who it was.

"You're mad." I eyed off the boarded-up door and shattered glass windows, shaking my head. "You cannot be serious."

Unlike so many of our generation, we'd returned to the Cove hoping to take advantage of the cheap housing and proximity to the beach. But jobs were few and far between, forcing us to travel over an hour each way to the bigger cities that sandwiched our tiny town.

"And you're not seeing the vision." She reached out to squish my cheeks between her hands, her eyes bugging out as she stared into mine.

"Close your eyes. Go on, close them."

I grinned; despite living in Astipia for over a decade, she'd never entirely lost her accent, her clipped London tone taking on a sharper bite when she experienced heightened emotions.

With a sigh born from a decade of friendship, I humored her, my eyelids drifting shut.

"Picture it, Ella," Anika whispered, her hands trembling against my cheeks. "A giant sign on the roof in beautiful bronze."

"That'll be expensive."

"Shh." She dropped her hands, and I could hear her moving around the lot as she articulated her vision. "Big windows at the front—with hurricane shutters, of course."

"Of course," I echoed, tongue in cheek.

Anika, predictably, ignored me. "A manicured entry with shrubbery and some beautiful metal ornaments."

The image she painted began to take shape in my mind.

"Inside, we create a wood and metal wonderland offset with rich colours and decadent fabrics."

"We'll need a bar," I murmured, picturing the space. "And a giant fireplace for winter."

"Absolutely!" Anika clapped her hands together, the sound loud in the quiet of the afternoon. "The doors will open outward for summer, and the lot will need to be cleared to host indoor-outdoor dining."

"We could do the food truck outside. Invite local and regional bands to play."

"Yes!" Anika's hands landed on my shoulders, squeezing. "And the kitchen will rival any in Paris, London, or New York."

I opened my eyes, considering the shambolic state of the building. "It's gonna be expensive." I tapped the food van behind me. "At least with Betsy, we don't have to worry about too many overheads. And we can shut her down or move around if there aren't any crowds."

"But don't you want more?" She swept a hand out to encompass the building. "We're not getting any younger—"

"Yes, twenty-five is horrendously old."

"—and opportunities like this don't come along every day."

I raised an eyebrow. "This place hasn't had

a tenant since before I was born. Why are you in such a rush now?"

She bounced from foot to foot, her long black hair shimmering like a waterfall. "Because of this." She shoved her phone back in my face, the smiling presenter still frozen on her screen.

"One TV show does not a success make."

"True." She tucked her phone away, throwing her hands out at the building. "But wouldn't you rather try than wonder 'what if'? What if this is the moment that tourists begin to flock to town? What if people decide that Astipia is *the* tourist destination this year? What if we're not prepared, and we lose out on what could be an awesome opportunity?"

I bit my lip, knowing Anika was right.

"But—" I gestured at our dismal surroundings. "How will we afford this? We're not just paying for a building. We're buying land and parking."

"There's a house out the back as well."

"And a house." I shook my head, a slight chuckle slipping free. "Ani, we're successful as a food van. We're able to afford a food van. This? It's a lot."

"I've already thought of it." She scurried to the van's cab, wrenching the door open and digging inside. "We'll capitalize on the millionaires!"

I rolled my eyes as she tripped, her legs flailing.

"Millionaires, I'm telling you. They're our future." She triumphantly held up a binder as she leapt from the cab. "We both know millionaires are sweeping in to buy up the private beaches over the other side of town. They're basically the only thing pumping money into the local area at the moment."

I crossed my arms, nodding.

"Well." She flipped open her binder with a flourish. "They're gonna need a nice place for dinner during their weekend vacays and business holidays." She handed me the binder. "And we'll be the answer to their hungry little prayers."

It was a business plan not unlike the one I'd handed her three years ago when I'd first floated the idea of a food van. We'd been commuting an hour each way to the city to work in jobs we hated for people we despised. The first year we'd lived in a one-room apartment with a horrible landlord who refused to pay for the hot water to be fixed. Despite the hardship, we'd made bank and eventually moved out to our own places.

"You even used the same font." I brushed a thumb over the thick paper. "Ani—"

"No time to get emotional." She tapped the paper. "It's all in here. Now, I know you don't want to use the money your grandma left you, but—"

My heart skipped, my head jerking up as I took in the building with new eyes.

Nan's money.

My inheritance had sat untouched for over a year. I'd been squirrelling it away for a rainy day, my grief tied to the money in my bank account.

"—but if we make it affordable and welcoming, even if it feels high class and caters to the VIPs, we can make a profit year-round." Anika pressed her hands together in a begging pose. "Please, Ella. Please say yes."

The rain that had threatened all day began to fall, the light patter dusting my cheeks and nose. I tilted my head back, staring at the cloudy sky.

Looks like my rainy day has arrived.

I closed my eyes, feeling at peace with my decision.

"All right," I told Anika, handing her the binder. "I'm in."

I couldn't be sure, but I highly suspected

that even the King, who lived over a thousand kilometres away, heard her scream of joy.

CHAPTER 1

Gunnar

Five years later

"Fuck." I tossed the wrench back into my toolbox, cursing the previous owner of this crap heap. "Double fuck."

I pulled my phone from my pocket, hitting my younger brother's number.

"Talk to me," Erik said, answering my call.

"It's fucked three ways to Sunday." I ran a grime-covered hand through my hair. "Blown gasket, oil pissing everywhere, there's rust in the crankshaft. It's a fucking mess."

"Damn." I could practically hear his brain

scrambling to fix the problem. "I guess you're gonna get a few days of forced leave after all."

Since my father had handed over the reins to our business five years ago, I hadn't taken a vacation. The company, its employees, and profits had to come first. The plans Erik and I made rested on our ability to deliver. As the eldest son and CEO, it was up to me to ensure we remained a success.

"If I didn't know better, I'd assume you planned this." I nudged the door to the engine room open with my foot, stepping into the doorway to watch the storm rage across the bow.

"I wish I had. I'd have ensured it sunk off the coast of a deserted island and forced you to take a real break for once."

I snorted as lightning lit up the marina, an immediate crack following the flash.

The storm had come on fast, the rough waves fucking with the already dodgy engine. I'd read the clouds early and steered for the closest port, a small marina in Capricorn Cove. The fucking thing had shit itself just as I'd docked.

"Sounds like a decent swirl," Erik said as thunder rumbled across the ocean and out to sea.

"She's a big'un, that's for sure." The boat

locked under my feet as waves battered her hull. Well used to the motion, I leaned into it, automatically adjusting to the flow. "I'm gonna hunker down here for the night. I'll assess the damage tomorrow and send you a parts order."

"Probably the best option. I'll mark this as holiday leave. Don't worry; Mac and Ian are more than capable of covering you."

I swore softly. "Sorry, bro."

"Don't sweat it. We'll add it to the client's bill. Just please, do me a favour. Try to relax a little?"

I snorted. "No promises."

Thunder interrupted his following comment.

"What was that?" I asked, pressing the phone closer to my ear.

"I said, where exactly are you?"

I glanced down toward the main marina, where an old, battered sign that had seen much, *much* better days sat peeling in the rain.

"Capricorn Cove."

"Sounds nice."

"I don't know about that." Another flash of lightning lit the sky, illuminating the mix of small fishing boats, millionaire yachts, and weekend dinghies.

"How about you call it a night? You eaten?"

"Not yet."

"Gunnar, it's after ten."

I glanced at my watch, silently cursing.

"Go wash up and get some food. Call me if you need anything?"

"Okay, *Mom*."

Erik chuckled down the line. "You fucker. Stay safe, okay?"

I blew out a breath. "Yeah, I'll try. Later."

"Later, Gunner."

I rinsed off the grease and grit, then donned a thick raincoat, turning up the collar as I searched for food.

Noting the time, I assumed my chances in a small town like Capricorn Cove wouldn't be good. But even a small town might have a motel or a late-night pizza joint.

I walked past a tattered For Sale sign hanging over the marina and boarded-up buildings before finding a path that led onto the main street. My initial impression of a run-down ghost town proved unfounded as I rounded the corner, surprised to find the street bustling with activity.

"Must be tourist season."

One bar caught my eye, the lights welcoming and the smell of smoked meat entirely too tempting when my damn stomach was already eating itself.

A surprisingly classy sign identified it as

The Bronze Horseman; the words hung above the door in a flourish of steel and light. Glass windows lined the well-lit and decorative entry, the car park a quarter full even at such a late hour. A couple walked out as I pushed the door open, bright-eyed and laughing as they rushed out into the storm, heading for their car.

The heavy wood door slammed behind me, muffling the thunder that rolled in a near-constant echo. I paused, taking in my surroundings.

Tasteful décor filled with rich woods, leathers, and bronze was offset by navy blue and hunter green highlights. It felt high-end but welcoming, a mix of homely and comfortable but luxurious.

A surprising contrast to the shit hole of a marina I'd just left behind.

A glance showed locals and tourists filled the booths and tables, the difference between the two easy to tell based on tan lines. The small groups chatted quietly or listened to the band on the far stage as they wrapped up their number.

A long bar dominated one wall of the restaurant; stools neatly tucked under the generous wood top. Two men were sitting at the far end closest to the gigantic fireplace; their heads bent together as they talked over a shared meal. Not in the mood for company, I slid onto a stool at the opposite end, snatching a menu from the closest stack, my eyebrows raising at the multitude of delicious options.

Maybe my luck had turned.

"What can I get you, Viking? Kitchen's open until midnight."

The words were delivered in the huskiest, sexiest voice I'd ever heard. My cock hardened, and I hadn't even seen the face that delivered that sucker punch.

I looked up to find full pouty lips, long lashes ringing satin brown eyes, soft, full cheeks, and big cascading brunette curls. My dick, already impossibly hard, pressed insistently against my fly.

Holy shit.

My gaze dropped, taking in her overly generous cleavage playing peek-a-boo with the v of her shirt.

Fuck.

The woman tilted her head, nodding at the menu in my hands. "See anything you like?"

"You." The word slipped free before I could stop it.

She laughed, sending that mass of hair shimmering. "I don't remember us adding me on there." She leaned forward, her shirt dipping to grant me a tantalizing glimpse of her lacy bra. "But for you? I'd consider making an exception." She winked, and I felt it deep in my gut.

Who'd have thought I'd be thanking the sea Gods for a busted engine?

"I'm Ella Bronze." She absently brushed a thick chunk of hair back. "And you are?"

"Gunnar Larsson."

Her cheeks flushed, a smile lighting her face. "Oh, I was right. You really are a Viking."

She's stunning.

At this rate, I'd be coming from one fucking smile. I grunted, shifting in my seat and grasping for any diversion. "What would you recommend?"

Ella leaned back over the bar, her tits pressing against the wood as she reached out to tap one of the menu items.

"Get the fully loaded burger. It's my favorite." She straightened, turning her back to me to bend over and pull a bottle from one of the beer fridges.

I want to bite her ass.

Big, curvy, and framed by thick thighs that I wanted clasped around my head while I licked her sweet cunt until she creamed on my tongue; she looked like fucking perfection.

I'd never had this kind of visceral reaction to someone before.

"Here." She popped the cap, sliding the beer across the bar. "On the house."

"Thanks." I eyed the label.

"Don't you trust me?"

"Of course." I sent her a wink. "Just like to know what I'm putting in my mouth." Tipping the bottle back, I took a long drag, the cider tart but refreshing as it burst across my tongue.

"Good?" she asked.

"Fucking perfect," I growled.

A wickedly seductive smile decorated her incredible lips. We both knew I hadn't been talking about the beer. One of the men down the far end called her name, interrupting our moment.

"Be right back," she promised.

I watched her sashay away, taking another long pull from the bottle. If I played my cards right, maybe I'd leave here with more than one hunger satisfied.

I lifted the beer again, drinking deep.

CHAPTER 2

Ella

H*e's here.*

I stood in the cooler, allowing the frigid air to calm my flushed cheeks as I tried not to freak out.

He's actually here!

"Don't be an idiot," I muttered to myself as I soothed my hands over my hair. "He's not here for you."

I closed my eyes, easily remembering how Gunnar—a stranger—had looked at me. His dark eyes practically devoured me as we chatted.

"Okay, Universe, is this the sign I needed?"

Thunder rumbled loudly above me as if in answer, the vibrations rattling the restaurant.

I huffed out a laugh. "I guess that might be a yes."

To some, it would seem strange that I was on the cusp of thirty and still a bona fide virgin. Oh sure, I had a nightstand full of sex toys, but I had yet to invite anyone into my bed. And really, I had no one to blame but myself for this sorry state of affairs.

For as long as I could remember, people in my life had made comments about my big thighs. Thunder thighs, they'd called them. Big, bold, and ready to crush the first man that dared to get between them.

I'd decided to own that narrative, laughing at the criticism and claiming I had thighs so mighty no mere mortal could lie between them.

My thighs could call down the God of Thunder.

My thighs were magic.

I owned thighs only a Viking God could plunder.

Maybe I'd bought into my own propaganda. Perhaps I'd been so caught up in the fantasy of a Viking God who adored every curve, dip, and cellulite-ridden stretch mark, that I'd lost sight of reality.

Either way, with three weeks until my thirtieth birthday, I'd decided to throw my pedestal man out the window and hit thirty as a recovering virgin.

Unfortunately, small towns weren't exactly hotbeds of single men. The ones I might have considered were married, the ones on the dating apps weren't interested in a fat woman, and the others were a bit too experienced or into kink for my first time.

I needed a man who would treat me with kindness, wanted my body, and knew how to make it sing.

I'd slowly given up hope but now?

He was here. My pedestal guy had finally arrived. And on a rumble of thunder no less. If that wasn't a sign, I didn't know what was.

I sucked in a breath, huffing it out slowly. "Am I really going to do this?"

I imagined spreading myself for Gunnar, allowing him to strip me naked and lay me down.

Warm desire pooled in my belly, my nipples sensitive against the soft cups of my bra, a wet heat slicking between my thighs.

My body says yes. My mind says yes. I guess yes, it is.

I took a deep breath, smoothing damp palms down my skirt.

"You got this, Ella. You're hot as fuck. You're sexy. You own this damn bar and have made it successful. You are confident, brilliant, and funny. If he doesn't want you, then it's his loss."

Or maybe he'll just throw you over the bar and eat you for dessert.

A shiver of anticipation raced down my spine.

I heard a bell on the other side of the cooler door, and Anika call, "Foods up."

"Got it!" I snatched a container of sliced lemons for the bar and exited the cooler. I shifted the container under one arm, lifting the warm plate piled with a burger, fries, and sauce with my free hand.

"Wait."

I turned back to see Anika wiggling her eyebrows, a knowing grin playing on her lips.

"Saw him. Like him, would do him." She tilted her head toward the bar. "You gonna take a chance on this one?"

I shrugged, offering her a coy smile. "Depends on if he likes our food."

She laughed, waggling a knife in my direction. "Correct answer. I'm not sure I can approve a cherry popper who doesn't know good food when it falls in his lap."

"Don't worry." I bumped the kitchen swinging door with my butt. "I've got a good feeling about him."

I dropped the lemon container on the back of the bar, taking a moment to breathe before heading toward the hottie at the far end.

You got this, Ella.

My belly flipped as I walked toward him. He nursed his beer, his warm gaze trained on me. Crackling awareness sparked between us, the restaurant narrowing until it was just this delectable man and me.

Now or never.

"Here you go." I slid the plate in front of him. "Enjoy."

He glanced down at the food, his eyebrows lifting.

"This is—"

"Delicious," I promised.

The burger contained three types of smoked meat, all cooked to perfection. Topped with melted cheese, pickles, onions, and delicious house mustard and ketchup, it looked, smelled, and tasted incredible.

In the months leading up to our opening four years ago, Anika and I had worked around the clock to develop the perfect menu, the best cocktails, and source the tastiest local beers.

Gunnar took a bite, and I watched as surprise decorated his face.

"Fuck," he muttered around a mouthful of meat. "This is *good*."

Moments like these made all those long nights and fraught decisions worth it.

One of my barmaids caught my attention.

"You need anything else?"

He shook his head at my question. "I'm good."

"I'll be right back." I turned away, trying to calm the thrum of anticipation that pulsed through my veins.

As the time ticked closer to close, I mixed drinks, cleaned the bar, and flirted with him between orders as I counted down each agonizing minute, praying he would stay.

Please stay.

He did, nursing a second beer while watching me with those knowing, dark eyes.

"He's still here," Anika murmured, filling her water bottle from the tap at the bar.

I ran my cloth over the sticky stainless-steel surface, determined not to glance at the man in question for the millionth time.

"Ella, in case you missed it, that's a good sign."

I flinched, unconsciously fisting the cloth. "Is it?"

"Abso-fucking-lutely." She nodded at the mostly empty restaurant. "How about you clock off and have a drink with Mister Viking? I can close up tonight." She tilted her head toward the opposite end of the bar where Drake Andrews and Dane Butler sat, mulling over papers spread around them. "As much as I want to be the meat in their sandwich, I'll take one for the team and do a little reconnaissance for our bestie."

I eyed the two men. "Did you text Blue?"

"As soon as they walked in," she confirmed. "The woman said she doesn't care, but we both know that's bullshit."

The two men had once lived in Capricorn Cove before joining the Navy. They'd been foster kids living with our friend, Bluebell 'Blue' McKenney. The three had been tight, permanently joined at the hip at parties or school. Until the men had enlisted and moved away, leaving Blue behind.

I rolled my eyes. "You're as subtle as a bull in a glass store."

"Lies! I'm the perfect spy. No one suspects a face this perfect to be so devious." She playfully spanked me on the butt. "Now go! Get out of here, woman, and get that man to introduce you to the delightful world of carnal desire."

I laughed, jumping away from her. "See you tomorrow."

"I want details!"

I grabbed my purse from storage and

sashayed my way out from behind the bar. Gunnar's dark eyes tracked me as I approached, a shiver of awareness dancing down my spine.

"Hey." I slid onto a barstool beside him, trying to calm my nerves. "You want some company?"

He smiled, lazy and slow. "Only if that company is you."

The spark that had cheerily crackled between us all night ignited. The fire of attraction undeniable. I broke eye contact, unused to anyone looking at me with such blatant want.

Anika plonked a beer on the bar with a grin before dancing away.

"Your friend?" Gunnar asked, nodding at Anika's retreating back.

"And business partner." I lifted the bottle and tipped it toward the kitchen. "I'm the beer wench; Anika's the one with the magic taste buds."

"Well, I can safely say this is one of the nicest bars I've ever stumbled into."

I arched an eyebrow. "Do you regularly stumble into bars?"

He leaned toward me, effortlessly bridging the gap between us. His scent teased my nose— salt, sweat, and a little musk.

"Only those with gorgeous owners."

Oof! This man is a danger to womankind.

Over a long drag of my beer, I locked my fill, taking in the broad cut of his shoulders, the barrel of his chest, his trunk-like legs. A mountain of a man, Gunnar made me feel dainty and small—no easy feat.

I'd been born curvy. My body built big, bold, and beautiful—and no amount of exercise or dieting was going to change my core shape. I'd learned to love my curves, accentuating them and finding pleasure in how my body moved and felt.

But my body wasn't in fashion—and was unlikely ever to be so. Which meant the Venn diagram representing the crossover between boys who wanted me and my attraction to them remained minuscule.

If I were honest, it appeared that only one name sat in the center of the chart tonight.

Perhaps it was the look in Gunnar's eyes, but I had a feeling he'd embrace my curves, showing them the love and appreciation I'd always longed for.

I cleared my throat, trying not to place too much hope on tonight. "So, tell me about yourself. What do you do?"

He grinned, slow and easy. "My brother and I co-own a boat building company.

Inherited it from our dad after he retired. Or, I should say semi-retired since he can't help himself."

I chuckled, enjoying the rueful affection with which he referred to his father. "Whereabouts?"

"Cape Hardgrave."

"Ah." I couldn't help but tease him. "So, you're a mainlander."

"Only when not on the sea."

We exchanged a smile. The friendly rivalry between the various islands of Astipia had been established centuries ago—we were simply a product of our upbringing.

I played with the label on my beer bottle. "A boat building company that must keep you busy."

"No more so that a bar, I imagine."

"Truth." I tilted my head. "I've never seen you around here before."

He leaned back, running a hand through his hair. "That's because I'm not normally this far north. We needed to pick up a yacht for a refurb, and no one else was available." He shook his head. "Should have known it'd be a cluster fuck when the client sent through the original refurb request."

I winced sympathetically. "That bad, huh?"

"The boat is barely functional. The storm kicked up and flooded the engine. I managed to baby her to the closest port, but it crapped itself as I docked. Expect I'll be here for a while waiting for some replacement parts to arrive." He rested his hand beside mine on the bar, one finger lightly running over my pinkie. His simple touch sent all my nerves firing, delicious pleasure settling low in my belly.

"Maybe the God of thunder was looking out for me."

I snorted. "Why do you say that?"

His big hand lifted to cup my cheek. He eased in, his mouth hovering a half hair from mine.

"Because I'm looking at a woman who I can only describe as a Valkyrie." His lips quirked. "Too corny?"

"A little, but in the nicest way."

"Good." His lips covered mine, his mouth firm but chaste.

What began as an exploration—the pressing of lips, his hand warm against my cheek, our knees grazing—quickly escalated. His lips seduced mine as he tilted my head, seeking better, deeper access. Our tongues tangled, his teasing mine in a wet, hot, and achingly demanding dance. I fell into a cloud of desire, asking for more, wanting more, desperate for him to take all I had to give.

He eased back, his eyes molten. "You wanna get out of here?"

I nodded, unable to speak.

"My yacht or your place?"

"Mine's closer," I answered without hesitation.

"Then lead on, Valkyrie."

The pet name turned my legs to jelly. I slipped from the barstool, leading him through the restaurant to the door.

The heavens again opened, torrential rain bucketing down as thunder and lightning crackled, electrifying the air.

It felt like a night to be reckless.

"Come on." I snatched Gunnar's hand, pulling him with a laugh into the downpour. We ran around the back of the bar and across the outdoor area to a gate at the far end of the property.

The rain fell in a violent torrent, washing away my inhibitions.

With a quick turn of my key, we stumbled down a gravel path, up three stairs, to pause on the stoop of the small cottage I called home.

My hand hovered over the doorknob.

"You're sure?" I asked, yelling to be heard over the crashing storm.

moment hadn't already been a life-changing event.

"Y-you want me to—?" I gestured to the bathroom.

"Oh, yeah." He turned to lean against the doorjamb. My gaze flicked down, noting that his wet clothes did nothing to conceal his arousal from me.

A crack of lightning outside briefly lit the interior of the house. Smashing thunder followed, so loud it rattled the frames on my wall.

Well, you heard the Gods.

This give and take remained unchartered waters for me. Kissing I could do. Heavy petting? Sure. Getting naked? Not so much.

I tried to inject careless confidence into my movement, brazening my way through.

Gunnar shifted, allowing me to pass by, our bodies grazing. He brushed a hand over my cheek and down my neck, lingering at my collar bone.

"Take it off," he ordered. "Strip for me, Ella."

I hesitated, wavering in my uncertainty.

"Please."

My hands dropped to my waist, pulling the shirt free of my skirt. Channeling confidence I wasn't sure I felt, I peeled the wet material from my body and tossed it aside, leaving me in a black bra that did magnificent things to my breasts.

Thank you for your choices, past Ella.

Gunnar huffed out a groan. "Now, the skirt."

I trembled as I fumbled with the zipper, drawing it down and pushing the material over my hips. The saturated fabric clung to my curves, forcing me to wiggle to get free.

Gunnar groaned, his gaze trained on my breasts.

"Fuck, you're gorgeous."

He moved, ripping his shirt free and tossing it in my bathtub. He shoved the jeans down his thighs with near violent movements, his cock falling to lay heavy against his thigh.

He wasn't wearing underwear.

Gunnar wasn't wearing underwear.

Omg! He wasn't wearing underwear!

Long and girthy, his cock suited his body shape, entirely in proportion with the rest of him.

"Bra," Gunnar barked, kicking free of his clothes. "Leave the underwear."

And just like that, I grew cognizant of the differences between us. Gunnar looked as if he were carved from stone. Beautiful and rugged with a timelessly raw brutality that made him all the more interesting. His sunkissed skin contrasted sharply with my pale pillowy abundance, my curvy softness beautifully lush against him.

I blinked. "Leave the—?"

"You want me to take you in the shower or bed?"

Delicious shimmers of pleasure sizzled through my veins, desire heating that hidden part of me.

"Bed," I whispered.

He reached out to run a finger across the top of my underwear. "Then you better leave these on." His lips quirked. "Not sure I'll be able to stop myself if you remove them."

A heavy, druggy feeling invaded my limbs —the sensation quite unlike anything I had experienced before as uncertainty, anticipation, and desire warred for supremacy.

Gunnar reached into the small shower stall, twisting the taps. He tested the temperature, adjusting it before gesturing for me to enter. I stepped past him, sighing as the warm water cascaded over my skin, chasing the slight chill away. He crowded behind me, dwarfing the space, his naked chest pressing against my back.

"I need a taste." His guttural groan sent shivers down my spine.

I moved to turn, but his hands fell to my hips, pinning me in place.

"No. Put your hands on the wall."

I complied, pressing my palms against the cool tiles, shifting to spread my legs.

"Good girl," he praised, one hand trailing down my spine. He adjusted the spray, so it fell down my back.

"Gunnar? I haven't done this before."

His hands, which had begun to draw slow circles up and down my back, paused. "Shower sex?"

"Any of this," I admitted, closing my eyes. "I'm a virgin."

He stiffened, falling silent.

I opened my eyes to stare at the tiles, heat flushing my cheeks. "Say something," I whispered.

"Do you want to sleep with me?"

"Yes."

"You want me to take your tight pussy?"

I shivered at his dirty words. "Yes."

He gripped my hips, pulling me back against him. His lips nipped at my ear lobe.

"Don't worry, baby." He gently tilted my chin so I could look at him. "I'll make this good for you."

He kissed me, rough, hard, hot. Our tongues tangled, wet and wanting as he took everything I had to give, offering me no escape, no option but to surrender.

I loved it.

He broke our kiss, pressing hot lips to my neck and shoulder. His hands seemed to be everywhere—trailing down my sides. brushing against my breasts, gripping the cheek of my ass.

I mewed, begging for something, anything —for *more*.

"Shhh," he whispered, nipping at my shoulder. "I'll give you what you need."

His hands slid over the soaked cotton of my underwear to hook underneath. His fingers, his clever, clever fingers, traced my outer lips, collecting evidence of my overwhelming arousal.

"What have we here?" His hot mouth brushed against my ear, pleasurable shudders wracking my body as he touched and teased. "Have you been a naughty girl, Ella?" He pressed against my naked pussy. "You do this for someone?"

"The B-Brazilian?" I asked. He ground his cock into my ass.

"Mm." He traced back and forth across the sensitive skin of my pussy with light. teasing fingers. I twitched under his hands, the glancing touches almost too much to bear.

"N-n-no." I stuttered, lost in the pleasure. "For me."

"Good answer."

I gasped as his fingers dipped, stroking me in a way no one ever had. He danced touches across my clit, pulling from me curses and praises in equal measure.

"More," I begged, pressing against his fingers. "Please, Gunnar. More."

He chuckled, the sound like dark chocolate and smooth whiskey. "I've got you, baby."

He removed his hand from my hip, sliding it up to play with my erect nipple. The other remained at my core; fingers teased my clit, tantalizing, dipping, dragging, corrupting me until I couldn't stand the spiraling tension.

"Please!"

He pressed hard against my clit, circling once, twice, a third time as I shattered under him, my cries filling the small stall as my body bowed, the orgasm sending me spiraling. I collapsed against the tile, legs unsteady, body shaking in the aftermath.

Gunnar soothed me with light kisses across my shoulder, his rough voice reassuring as he held me tight against his chest. "I've got you, baby."

I pressed my cheek against the tiled wall, struggling to find my way back to reality—my new reality. The reality where a man had pulled from me with skillful fingers and little effort, something I had only ever done for myself.

He switched the water off, holding me until I could stand.

"Let me help you."

He ran a towel over himself, wrapping it low around his hips before he turned back to me. Batting my hands away, he grazed the fluffy fabric over my skin, backtracking to ensure he caught every drop of water. With gentle hands wrapped my hair, long, thick, and heavy with water, in another towel, pressing kisses along my shoulder as he did.

I allowed him to look after me, letting him move me in whatever direction he desired. I'd never had anyone look after me like this—the feeling both intoxicating and arousing.

He pulled back, taking my hand. "Where's your bed—"

My stomach rumbled, interrupting him.

"Hungry?" Gunnar asked, his lips twitching in amusement.

"Busy shift and we were down a person. I might have skipped dinner," I admitted. "Normally, I'd just grab something after we closed, but...."

"But I interrupted your plans."

I laughed, leaning into his chest. "That's not to say it wasn't a welcome interruption."

He pulled me close, pressing a soft kiss to the tip of each breast.

"Get dressed. I'll see what I can rummage up for you."

I gave into impulse, catching his head to hold him against my breasts, delighting in the feel of his stubble rasping against my skin. "How about you go into the bedroom and wait for me while I—"

"Nope." He pulled back, brushing his knuckles over my cheek. "I have a rule, Ella. A woman lets me into her bed; the least amount I can do is feed her and make sure she enjoys herself."

His hand dropped to palm one of my breasts. "We've done half of the latter. It's time for you to allow me to do the former."

I sucked in a shuddering breath, heat again beginning to pool in my abdomen.

"Gunnar...."

He stepped back. "Let's get you fed before I lose my mind."

Heart in my throat, I rewrapped the towel around myself and allowed him to lead me from the bathroom—mentally asking myself the one question I wasn't sure I wanted to answer.

Could this night be any more perfect?

sourdough bread, dipping them into the liquid and then laying them flat on a heated pan.

"That smells good," Ella said, moving toward me. I paused mid-flip, my mouth watering as I drank her in. She'd dried her hair, letting it fall freely around her face in a messy tangle. She wore a printed kimono, which she'd left untied at the front. Under the robe lay a black slip of lace and satin, which clung provocatively to her every dip and curve.

Fuck breakfast. I wanted to taste every inch of her.

"What?" She glanced down, hands hovering above her stomach. "Do I have something on here? I had to pull it out of storage. I'm not normally a lingerie sort of girl, so it may have some dust—"

I pulled her into me, my mouth silencing hers. She fell into the kiss, letting me take what I needed, willingly following me down any path I chose. This level of trust—of blind innocence—was a heady, powerful thing.

And so goddamned humbling. I wanted this to be good for her. Wanted her to enjoy every moment. I needed to make this perfect.

I'd never believed in love at first sight. Hell, I hadn't even been convinced that love really existed. But this pull between us was undeniable. The longer I spent with her, the

CHAPTER 3

Gunnar

I heard Ella moving in her bedroom while I dug through her pantry and fridge. The candles around the house filled the space with warm, flickering light. Outside, the storm continued to rage, thunder and lightning locked in combat.

Ella's pantry was surprisingly well stocked—though I should have expected a restaurant owner to be a foodie who loved to cook.

I laid my ingredients on her kitchen island, settling on a breakfast dish. I whisked eggs, cinnamon, vanilla, milk, and a pinch of sugar together, pouring the wet mix into a flat pan. Putting it aside, I sliced thick pieces of more I became convinced that this wasn't just lust or infatuation. Ella made me consider things I hadn't ever turned my mind to before. Things like maybe these feelings between us weren't simply sexual.

Could I have found my soul mate? Did I even believe in soul mates?

The fact was, I'd known this woman less than four hours, and here I stood in her kitchen considering the possibility of settling down, of making a life here with her.

My family would laugh themselves silly if they could see me right now. I wasn't exactly known as Mister Love. Workaholic, decisive, stoic? Yep.

The kind to fall head-over-heels for a woman I'd just met? Fuck no.

I broke our kiss, returning to the stove just in time to rescue the toast.

"What are you making?" Ella asked, wrapping arms around my middle.

"French toast with maple bananas."

"Can I help?"

"Sure, can you slice the banana?"

She pressed a kiss to my back before moving to the kitchen island. We worked in companionable silence for a few minutes, me cooking the toast, her slicing and transferring the bananas to the waiting pan.

"One minute on each side," I explained, flipping the toast slices. "Then we'll coat with a generous glug of maple, and it'll be done."

"Glug, huh?" She leaned her hip against the counter beside me, her stunning eyes warm with amusement. "Is that an official measurement?"

I chuckled. "Oh ye of little faith. Just you wait."

I held up the maple bottle, tipping it over the pan. An air bubble formed in the neck and bubbled up, making a glug sound as the liquid squeezed past.

"No way!" Ella exclaimed, slapping my arm playfully. "That's ridiculous."

"It's a Viking trade secret," I told her solemnly, holding the spatula to my chest. "We only divulge it to the noblest of Valkyries."

She laughed, her stunning eyes dancing with mirth. "I swear to take it to my grave."

I divided the food, decorating the toast with the caramelized banana pieces. We sat at her breakfast bar, digging into the syrupy mess.

"Oh, God," Ella groaned, closing her eyes. "This is divine. I should add it to our menu."

I grinned, enjoying her pleasure. "You're welcome. It's not every day I get to feed a beautiful woman."

She tipped to head to one side, considering me as she chewed.

"What?" I asked, slicing into the toast with my fork. "What's that look?"

"I guess I just realize I know nothing about you. You say it's not every day, yet I wouldn't know if that were true."

I laid down my fork and reached for her free hand, entwining my fingers with hers. Turning fully toward her, I leaned in, catching and holding her gaze.

"It's true. Contrary to what tonight might seem, I'm not someone who sleeps around. It's been—" I paused, trying to remember the last time I'd hooked up with someone. "—a while. And before that, it was a relationship that lasted a year." I leaned my forehead against hers. "This attraction between us? It's hot as fuck and is making me lose all my cool."

"I don't know whether to be happy about that."

I pulled back, slowly letting her go. "You can tell me after I make you come multiple times."

She blushed, dropping her head to her plate and shoveling food in her mouth. Grinning at her reaction, I changed the subject.

"Have you always lived in Capricorn Cove?"

Ella nodded. "My mother's family traces our line back to the original Manari tribes. They were fishermen and women who settled in this area, living off the land and sea until the colonizers arrived. Later some became farmers while others chose the sea."

"And your father's side?"

"A Hodge podge mix of Europeans who washed up on Astipia's shores." She chuckled, spearing a banana piece. "My father's people are *not* sailors. They're mostly academics from way back. I think we even have a former priest in the mix."

"And you've never thought of leaving?"

"Absolutely not. This is my home. This is where I feel connected to country and family."

I understood the sentiment. "My mother's people are from America and, before that, Europe. But my father's are from Norway. We're able to trace his line back to the Vikings. I went to Norway for work a few years back, and stepping onto the country that ran so deep in my DNA felt like coming home. Like I'd connected to a piece of myself I didn't know was missing."

"Exactly!" She pointed her fork at me, her eyes sparkling. "It's why I don't think I'll ever leave. I love it here. There's so much beauty and history. Astipia itself is a land rich in culture, but Capricorn Cove?" She shook her head. "It's glorious."

"I'm beginning to see the appeal."

Our conversation roamed freely and easily as we ate, and despite the desire humming through my veins, I found myself loathed to rush us to the bedroom. Ella delighted the hell out of me and learning more about her simply increased my attraction.

I'm in over my head.

"I attended Norwell, I got my business degree, then got the hell out," I told her. "I fucking hated college. Hated studying. I'm better when I can act on what I know—being forced to learn without any outcome? It's like torture to me. You?"

"Community college. It's about an hour from here. Even a few years away would have been too many."

I nodded. "What did you study?"

"Hospitality and business." She grinned. "I always knew I wanted to make a go of it here. People are searching for the quaint, quiet spots they remember from childhood—but with all the amenities they expect as an adult. We started with a food van, but after my grandmother passed and left me some money, Anika convinced me to invest it."

"Sorry for your loss."

"Thank you." She offered me a small smile. "I still miss her, but I think she'd be proud of what we've built." She leaned forward, her slip dipping just enough to reveal the shadow of her nipples. "And she loved this town. The ocean, the people. I think she'd adore that I'm creating a life for myself here."

"I feel you," I replied, ignoring my cock that now tented the towel I wore. "I'd get home every chance I got. I grew up on boats and beaches. It felt like a part of me was missing while living on campus."

"Lake Muniahra didn't do it for you?" she teased, reaching out to squeeze my knee.

I captured her hand, entwining her fingers with mine. "I doubt anyone would think the lake was a substitute for a great beach." I rested our hands on the towel covering my thigh. "So, what's next for you? Expansion?"

"Actually, the property is so large that this year we've been doing brunch in the yard on weekends. It's taken off enough to justify opening for lunch and breakfast next year in addition to the evening hours. We're beginning to see more competition with new places opening, but we're tried and true with a stellar reputation." She laughed. "Not to mention the local connections to get all the best produce."

I chuckled. "Nothing like some good local nepotism."

"Absolutely! I'm also toying with the idea of buying a few more properties. There are three along the cliff road—all outdated and needing repairs—but their owners are getting on and thinking of selling. They have amazing views, which would be a real selling point. I was considering maybe snapping up a few and doing them up as holiday homes. Offering them with a package deal for weddings."

"Well, shit. You're a Queen building an empire." I pressed a kiss to the back of her hand.

She flushed but didn't look away. Our gazes caught, holding, the relaxed atmosphere giving way to crackling tension.

"Ella." I ran my thumb over the back of her hand.

"Yeah?"

"Get on the counter."

Her eyebrows rose. "Excuse me?"

"Hop up on the counter, baby."

"But." She tilted her head to one side, a thick chunk of her hair falling over her shoulder. "Why?"

I slid off my stool, pulling my towel free with one tug. My cock sprang up, ready and rearing to go. "Because I want to eat your pussy."

Her gaze dropped to my cock. Her lips parted, her eyes glazing over.

Fuck yes. This is one hell of a woman.

I was about to lose my patience and lift her onto the counter when she slid off her chair and sank to her knees.

"Ella, what are you—?"

"I wanna taste," she murmured, reaching a hand out to my cock. She hesitated, glancing up at me. "Is this okay?"

"Fuck yes." It took all my goddamned willpower to keep from reaching for her. "You do whatever makes you feel good—whatever you want."

I fucking loved that Ella had taken one look at me and liked what she saw. It drove me wild to know that she wanted me in her mouth, the taste of me on her tongue.

I watched as she settled on her knees, her hand wrapping around the base of my cock as she considered me. She licked her lips, a slight frown in place.

"Okay, baby?" I asked, tensing.

"Yeah, just—working it out," she muttered.

"Working—" I broke off, a mangled groan bursting from my throat as she leaned forward, taking hold of me in one quick slide. The heat of her mouth, the drag of her tongue, the warmth enveloping my cock—all of it was fucking incredible.

Valhalla. Heaven. Nirvana.

I didn't care what name you assigned to this pleasure. All I knew was I never wanted this to end.

Ella drew back, one hand reaching up to brush hair from her face.

"Let me," I grunted, wrangling movement from my pleasure-soaked body. I reached down, fisting her hair, and pulling it back from her face. She moaned as my fingers delved into her thick mass, massaging her scalp.

"You like that?" I asked, testing the waters a little.

"So much," she panted, licking her lips.

I pulled at her hair with my fist, just enough to add a small bite of tension.

Ella groaned, her eyes closing as she enthusiastically surged forward against my pull, mouth desperately sucking me back in.

It seemed as if my woman liked a little pain with her pleasure.

She's fucking perfect.

She sucked and swallowed, her hand stroking the base of my cock while her lips and tongue drove me crazy. There was no finesse to her movements, no practiced artifice to take away from her enthusiasm. This was raw, desperate need.

And I fucking loved every moment.

She pulled back, tonguing my crown to find a sensitive spot on the underside of my cock.

"Fuck," I panted, holding her head still as my hips jerked, my cock thrusting in and out of her willing mouth. "Gonna come, baby. Tap my leg if you want me to pull out."

She didn't. She kept up her pace, hungry, wanton sounds escaping her throat.

"Fuck!" I exploded into her mouth, cum hitting the back of her throat. She swallowed it down with a small hum of pleasure.

"Jesus Christ," I collapsed back on the stool, hand stroking her hair. "Fuck."

Ella giggled, rising to her feet. She stumbled, and my hands shot out to grip her hips to steady her.

"That was—" She bit her lip, searching for the words. "Beautiful."

"Yeah." I grinned, pulling her in close to nuzzle her cheek. "I have to agree. You looked pretty fucking gorgeous with my cock down your throat."

I felt the blush heat her cheek.

"Gunnar!"

"What?" I pulled back, one hand following the curve of her body to graze over her abdomen and down to the seam of her pussy. I slipped a hand under her lingerie, finding her naked and soaked. My fingers captured her wet heat, the musky smell of her desire driving me crazy.

Finding her clit, I drew lazy circles around the sensitive flesh, loving her gasped moan. Her nails dug into my forearm, her body arching as she searched for more.

"You ever do that for anyone else?"

She shook her head, her hips shifting restlessly against my hand. Arrogant satisfaction settled in my gut.

I would be her first everything. Her final too, if I had my way.

I shoved that last thought aside, unable to process the possessive instinct that drove me to lay claim to this woman.

"I think that effort deserves a reward, baby," I murmured, increasing the pressure against her clit. Her hands gripped my arms, her mouth parting as tiny mews escaped.

I kept her like that, imprisoned between my thighs, one hand pressing her to me, the other delivering pleasure.

"Ready?" I asked, my lips pressed to the shell of her ear.

She nodded, frantic in her search for an ending to this exquisite torture. I tugged at her slip dress, sliding the material down over her breasts until they spilled free. I moved in, pressing hot kisses to her nipples, sucking them into my mouth to tongue her.

Desperate pleas began to spill from her lips, filthy demands for more.

I shifted my fingers a fraction up and to the right, finding a spot that drove her wild.

Ella shattered, her legs imprisoning my hand as her cries filled the house, her body convulsing as she coated my fingers in her cream.

"Fuck," I muttered, letting her ride out her orgasm. My cock hardened against my thigh, a bone-deep hunger taking up residence in my gut.

Ella trembled against me, her breath short and sharp.

"Shhh, baby," I whispered, brushing comforting hands along her back. I pulled the slip back up, hiding her glorious tits from my view. "Just breathe."

"I've never—that was—" She shuddered.

"I know." I pressed a kiss to her forehead, her cheek, tilting her head up to reach her lips. "Just breathe."

We stayed there for a long moment, wrapped in each other. I prayed to the Gods that she felt the same mix of crazy emotions I did. Fucking hell, if I was the only one feeling this way.... At this point, I'd be ready to raze this town to the ground for her if she asked.

You need to dial it down a notch. This is fucking ridiculous.

Ignoring the sensible voice in my head, I drew back a fraction to look down at the gorgeous woman in my arms.

"Bed?" I asked.

"Please."

CHAPTER 4

Ella

Having each snagged a candle to light our way, I led Gunnar to my bedroom. The pause gave me just enough time to rationalise the last few hours.

I theoretically knew I should be nervous with the way this night was progressing, but I couldn't seem to conjure up an ounce of anxiety or concern. Perhaps I was overly naïve or blinded by a flood of endorphins; either way, this felt right.

The man knew how to kiss. He could play me like a dream. He pulled reactions and feelings from me I hadn't even known were possible. And believe me, I'd spent years and thousands of dollars cultivating a vibrator collection worthy of its own museum.

Despite all we'd done, I was still a virgin. At this point, I could probably ask him to put his clothes on and send him on his way, both of us satisfied with the evening's events.

But I didn't want to. I wanted this man— this funny, attractive man who made me food and played my body to perfection.

It wasn't like I hadn't had offers over the years. A few guys had asked me out; fewer still had made it to a second date. Only one had ever interested me enough to make it to date number three, though any attraction between us had died following a dinner date that went sour.

Some might think I was picky, but I'd spent a lifetime learning to love my curvaceous, beautiful body, and I didn't need anyone convincing me otherwise. I was fabulous— utterly incredible, and no man, especially not a man I was considering letting into my life, had the right to tell me otherwise.

I led Gunnar to my bedroom, shuffling to a halt at the foot of my bed. I set the hurricane glass on the bedroom bench, the battered wood from my grandmother's hope chest catching the warm, flickering candlelight. Outside, the rage of the storm had passed. While rain continued to fall, the violence of the thunder had retreated to a rumble in the far distance, the sound comforting rather than electrified.

Gunnar placed the second candle holder on my bedside table, glancing around the room.

I tried to see the design through his eyes, wondering what he thought of the white walls and soft pastel furnishings. I'd gone for a feminine, beach, boho feel. Wood and glass mixed with soft fabrics, plants, and meaningful knickknacks to make the room both comfortable and cozy.

"You a designer?" he asked, lifting a photo that sat on my bedside table.

"No, I just like pretty things."

In contrast to the elegant, feminine energy, Gunnar dominated the space. His raw masculinity in no way diminished by the overtly female palette.

He returned the photo frame to its place. "Looks real nice."

My heart skipped just a little, pleased by his praise. "It's not very big. But I try to make sure every room has a personality. A different feel."

"And this one is a warm hug?" he asked, walking around, fingers brushing the scarves I'd hung beside the window.

"I guess that's as good a description as any."

He pulled one long scarf free, running the silk across his palm. He turned to me, a thoughtful expression on his face.

"Have you ever thought about how you want your first time to go?"

My breath caught in my throat, my pulse jumping.

Only a million times.

As a young girl, I'd imagined a wedding followed by a night of sweet kisses—fairytales didn't generally reveal what happened after the clock struck twelve. As a teen, I'd imagined hot kisses leading to a rose-covered bed or a clashing of mouths so passionate we'd only make it as far as the backseat of a car. As an adult, I'd fantasized about one-night stands and men with whom I'd form immediate connections. They'd whisk me away to their hotel room, showering me with passion. Once, I'd even considered attending a sex club in the city, of offering myself up to whoever wanted me. I'd be blindfolded, letting myself be taken by the person my mind created rather than subjected to the disappointment of reality.

"Yes," I finally whispered, my heart thumping loudly in my ears.

"And?" Gunnar asked, pulling the silk across his palm again. His movements were slow, deliberate, almost hypnotic. If one could

I slowly raised my hands, running them over the soft skin of my thighs, dragging fingers across the curves of my stomach, up to briefly cup my breasts. I rolled my thumbs over my nipples, pleasure sparking at both the tease of my fingers and his look of barely contained desire.

"Up. Now!" he ordered, reaching for my hands.

I complied, lifting my arms and holding them above my head. He placed a knee on the bed, leaning over me to wrap the scarf around my wrists.

"You say no, I'll stop," he promised, threading the scarf into a decadent cuff. "You pull on this," he placed an end in the palm of my left hand. "The knot will fall apart. The first rule is to trust you are always safe." He pressed a kiss to my wrist. "You feel safe, baby?"

I nodded, unable to answer, thanks to my heart relocating to my throat.

Silly heart. He's here for the night, not forever.

"Good." He stepped back, his gaze caressing the shape of me. He reached down, lazily fisting his cock. "Spread your thighs, Ella."

I slowly dragged my legs open, watching as Gunnar's expression changed. The naked desire there shifted, growing hungrier, needier.

"Like this?" I spread wider, revealing myself to him fully.

"Fuck," the word tore from him, almost violent in its intensity. "Stay there."

He rounded the bed, dropping to his knees. Reaching across, he hooked his arms under my knees and hauled me over to the edge. I let out a squeal as his head dropped to my crotch, his lips and tongue playing cross my seam.

"Oh, God." I arched against his mouth as his tongue dipped, sweeping across my clit. The scarf pulled against my wrists, reminding me of my helplessness as I shifted restlessly.

"Good girl," he murmured, pulling back slightly to press a kiss to my thigh. "I got you, Ella."

His mouth returned, and he played me like an expert musician. A slow set of circles, a slight suction, a finger pressed just so. I sighed in pleasure, moaning, eyelids drifting shut as he built me up, again and again, never letting me tip over the edge.

"Please," I begged, my body writhing under his mouth. "Gunnar—"

He chuckled against me, the vibrations hitting my core. With a tiny shift he pressed a

finger against my entrance as his tongue worked my clit in a pattern designed to drive me crazy.

"Gunnar!" I gasped his name, hips arching as I crashed into my orgasm. I fell apart, my body shuddering and quaking until I was left limb with spent need.

Gunnar shifted, resting his chin on my abdomen. Drowsily I blinked my eyes, peeking at him from beneath lowered lashes. I loved the smile that pulled at his lips, the contentment that settled in the lines of his face. He looked—satisfied. Happy.

"Hey," he murmured, his tone gentle. "You good?"

"Joyfully perfect." I stretched, the scarf pulling at my wrists. "Oh. I'm still—"

"I got you." Gunnar pushed up, crawling slowly up the bed, dragging lazy kisses across the dips and planes of my body. He hesitated his fingers on the scarf. "You want me to let you go, or are you ready for more?"

I shivered, bumps rising across my skin. "More?"

"Mhmm. We're just getting started." He reached down to slip naughty fingers between my legs. "You feel ready."

I whimpered as he played, pleasure shimmering up my spine.

"You ready for me to be inside you, baby?" He nipped at my collar bone as one of his hands cupped my breast, thumb grazing across my nipple.

"Yes," I breathed, arching into his touch. "Yes."

He chuckled. "You sure? You ready for me to fill this tight cunt?" His fingers pressed deeper, eliciting an exquisite sense of stretched fullness.

I squirmed, reaching down to grasp his cock in my hand. He grunted, eyes hovering at half-mast.

"In me. Now," I demanded. I pulled him toward me, careful not to displace the condom my lust-filled brain hadn't even registered him rolling on.

Gunnar followed my lead, allowing me to guide him to my core.

"Ready, Ella?" he asked, positioning himself just so.

"Yes."

He pushed forward, stretching me in a way that felt strangely beautiful despite the pain.

A double-edged sword. Pleasure and pain in equal measure.

He eased in, allowing me ample time to adjust.

"Okay?" Gunnar asked, his breath whispering against my cheek.

"Oh, yes," I murmured, closing my eyes. "It feels—"

Painful. Wonderful.

"Full."

He laughed, groaning when I moved under him. "Steady, or this will be over before it even begins."

He pressed kisses to my cheeks, and my lips, sucking gently at my neck before shifting down to trace a path to my breasts. He laved one, then the other, drawing them into his mouth and sucking on my overly sensitive nipples.

I shifted, my lips reaching up to press hot, wet kisses to any part of him within reach. My hands looped over his neck, clinging as best I could while bound. He nestled between my thunder thighs as if he belonged there.

Maybe he does...

He began to move, thrusting slowly into me, moving with certainty. My body had adjusted to his size and shape, accommodating him, welcoming him in with a heated grasp.

"You feel so good, baby," he murmured against my shoulder. "Amazing. Tight. Hot. So fucking incredible. So fucking good."

"Your cock is—" I didn't know how to describe it.

He quickened his pace, shifting slightly to change the angle.

"Ohmigod," I bowed off the bed, eyes rolling into the back of my head as he hit a perfect spot.

"Again," I demanded, greedy for more. "Again!"

He obliged, his thrusts steady and sure, quickening at my gasping pleas.

"Please, please, please—"

He grunted, shifting to move a hand between us. His fingers delved, searching for—

"Fuck!" I screamed, my body shattering into a million pieces as he pressed hard, urgent circles against my clit. "Gunnar!"

He swore, continuing to thrust into me with the same urgency and purpose. Even as I broke apart—this orgasm ruining me for any battery-powered assistance in the future—Gunnar powered through, our gazes locked as he guided my release, his attention trained solely on me.

I couldn't help but be seduced by the intensity of his focus.

I tugged the scarf, freeing my hands so I could knit my fingers in his hair. With a rough jerk, I pulled his head down to mine, desperate to taste him. Our lips locked, our mouths hungrily devouring each other as he continued to thrust into me, the perfect glide of his thick cock building me up again.

"Gunnar," I panted between kisses. "Come for me."

His pace kicked up, his grunts and praises coming faster as his control shattered. He drove into me, bottoming out, my bed thumping rhythmically against the wall while outside thunder rolled in the distance.

Mine. My man. Mine.

I moaned under him, another orgasm building.

"Gunnar—"

"Come for me," he demanded harshly. "Come on, my cock, Ella."

I broke, crying out as my body tightened, clenched, and spasmed. He muttered filthy, dirty words, cursing and praising as I drifted away, lost in sensation.

"Fuck, Ella!" Gunnar shuddered, his cock jerking in me as he came.

He rode out his climax, collapsing onto me with a groan. We breathed together, sweat cooling on our skin as my heart continued to race.

Gunnar twisted, raising slightly to look down at me. "Okay?"

"Oh, yes," I whispered, offering him a small smile.

He shifted onto one elbow, his eyes warm and affectionate. "Let's get you cleaned up; then I'll try again."

I cocked an eyebrow, a smile playing at the corners of my mouth. "Again?"

"Baby, you're no longer a virgin. But missionary is only one position." He pressed a kiss to the tip of my breast. "There's a whole universe of positions to explore."

I hesitated. "Tonight or...?"

He paused. "Definitely tonight." He reached out to brush a curl from my cheek. "And for as long as I'm in town—if you'll let me."

My heart seized at the reminder this was temporary.

You knew that going in. Don't let your unrealistic expectations ruin what is a beautiful experience.

I sucked in a breath, forcing a smile.

"You know...." I let my eyelids drop to half-mast, my legs falling open. Sliding a hand down my body, I trailed fingers through the wet heat pooled at the juncture of my thighs. "I do have one or two positions I've thought about before."

Gunnar's head drooped, watching as I played with myself. "Yeah?"

"Mmm." I slid a finger up, dancing around my over-sensitized clit. "Doggy, for one."

"We can try that." His voice dropped to a husky whisper.

"Girl on top."

"Definitely on the list."

"Against a wall—"

He shoved my fingers out of the way with a growl. "Cock tease."

Giggles of giddy delight spilled out of me like bubbles in a champagne bottle as he dropped to his back, hauling me over him. He tore the first condom free, quickly disposing of it before rolling another down his cock.

"Let me eat you. Then you're gonna ride my cock."

I hesitated, glancing down.

"What?" he asked, his hands stilling. "Too sore?"

"No, it's just...." I slapped my thighs. "What if I squish you?"

A grin stole across his lips, his eyes sparkling with mischief. "Then I'll die a happy man."

With that, he hauled me up his body, settling me over his face, his tongue wasting no time driving me wild.

I gripped the bed head, rocking against his talented mouth until I came.

"Good girl," Gunnar praised, his hands gripping my thighs. "Now ride my cock, baby."

Oh, but I was more than happy to oblige.

I shuffled down, settling over him. My thick thighs framed his body, pressing into his sides. Allowing him to help, I guided his cock to my core.

"Slow, baby," he murmured as I sank down. "Good girl, take my cock, baby. Take me deep."

I whimpered, eyes shutting at the feel of him filling me up.

"That's it." His hands stroked up my sides, soothing me. "Easy, baby. Easy. No rush. Take your—"

He jerked, a strangled groan ripped from his throat as I slammed down, forcing his cock into me.

"Shit," I jerked up. "Sorry, I—"

He held me in place, his hands framing my hips. "Keep fucking going."

I repeated the same move, both of us gasping at the delicious friction.

"Baby," he grunted, arching under me. "You feel so fucking good. You keep this up, and I'm gonna come."

I rolled my hips, finding far more pleasure in this position than I'd ever imagined. He didn't act like I was too heavy or big. He looked at me with desire, his hands caressing inches of skin I never thought a man would touch.

"Am I—"

"You're perfect," he interrupted. "You feel fucking amazing. You look like a goddess riding my cock." He squeezed my thighs with his hands. "You just keep going, baby. Keep making us both feel good."

I gave in to the primal rhythm of my body. My hands drifted from where they rested on his chest, dragging lazily up my torso to cup my breasts, my thumbs running slow circles over my erect nipples.

"Fuck yeah," Gunnar grunted, his hands gripping my hips. "Tease your beautiful tits. Pull those gorgeous nipples. That's it. Good girl."

I shuddered around him, a low moan slipping free.

"You like that?" he asked, shifting under me. He held me in place, holding me captive as he took over, fucking into my body with deliberate strokes. Over and over his cock hit me deep and steady, as if he were a warrior come to plunder.

"You want more of me?" he demanded. "You want more of this? You wanna come for me, my good girl? Beg for it, baby. Tell me how much you want it."

"Please, Gunnar. Fuck me. Fuck me!"

He thrust once, twice and we both came in a flash of curses. Utterly spent, I fell onto his chest, both us panting as we fought for breath.

His arms enveloped me, holding me tight against him as he dragged a hand slowly up and down my back over and over.

"Wow," I murmured, my eyelids still closed.

"I second that," he replied, pressing soft kisses to my shoulder.

We lay recovering in silence for long moments, our breathing evening out.

Rolling me gently, Gunnar shifted off the bed. "You rest, baby." He pressed a kiss to my shoulder. "I'm just gonna get rid of these condoms."

I listened as he moved around, fighting the druggy pull of sleep.

He returned with a warm washcloth, and tried to clean my thighs.

"No, I got this." I gently pushed his hand away, a flush heating my skin.

"You sure? I love taking care of you."

I pushed up from the bed. "I'm good. Thank you though."

I went to the bathroom, finding traces of blood on my thighs.

"To quote Anika, a cherry well popped."

Using the warm washcloth I cleaned the traces of the nights activities from my body. mentally checking in with myself.

Am I okay?

I watched myself in the mirror as I brushed my teeth. I didn't know why I expected to look different. But the woman in the mirror—apart from the flushed cheeks, messy hair, and well kissed lips—looked no different.

But I am. I've finally done it. And honestly, why did I wait this long?

I didn't want to admit that maybe, just maybe, I'd been waiting for Gunnar.

I returned to the bed, listening as Gunnar checked the laundry, setting the dryer for another cycle. I heard him moving around the house—no doubt blowing out the last of my candles and locking my doors, before returning to the bedroom.

In the soft glow of the remaining candle, he slipped back into bed, pulling me into his chest.

"All good?" I asked.

"Clothes are still wet but should be fine by tomorrow," he replied softly, moving me until I was the little spoon to his big one.

I'd never spooned with a man before. It felt both overwhelmingly claustrophobic and beautifully comforting.

"Okay?" he asked.

"Um, maybe?"

He chuckled. "Don't worry, you'll get used to it."

My ass settled against his crotch while his hand shifted to my side. His fingers glided across my skin. I relaxed, lulled by the hypnotic pattern and the heat of him at my back.

Okay, *this* I could live with.

CHAPTER 5

Ella

I woke to a tangle of sheets and an empty bed. Sunlight streamed through the crack in my curtains, the room already hot and sticky thanks to the increased humidity the storm had left behind.

Straining, I listened for movement in my house, hearing nothing but the ocean in the distance and the call of seagulls outside.

For a moment, I wondered if I'd dreamed Gunnar. If last night had been a beautiful figment of my imagination.

I shifted, feeling a slight ache between my legs.

Definitely not a dream.

I quickly walked around my house, double checking each room. My initial sense was correct—Gunnar was gone.

Suppressing the disappointment, trying valiantly to look on the bright side, I showered, washing his scent from my skin.

In an effort to shake off my funk, I threw on a summer dress, pulling my hair back into a messy, wet bun. Standing before my mirror, I examined the woman staring back. Her lips were swollen and dark smudges coloured the skin under her eyes, while her cheeks were tinted pink—from residual pleasure or beard burn, I wasn't sure.

"No regrets," I whispered. "No matter what happens, you gave yourself freely and without restraint. You enjoyed Gunnar and he enjoyed you. He worshipped your body, and you rocked his world. Don't dwell. You're gorgeous, fierce, and a complete badass. If he doesn't realise that, then that's his loss. But don't you dare regret a moment of this." I gave myself a firm nod, mentally dressing in my Wonder Woman costume.

I'm a sexy badass. I can do this.

My phone buzzed, a notification from my book club popping up on the screen. Unlocking the cell, I read over the messages I'd missed last night, a flush creeping up my neck.

ANIKA

LADIES! ELLA PICKED UP!
THIS IS NOT A DRILL! ELLA
PICKED UP!!

COLLINS

No fucking way!

HONEY

Yes Queeeeeeeen!! Finally!!

BLUE

Do we know him? Who is this
pillar of godliness?????

ANIKA

A customer. Never seen him
before. Picture big broad
shoulders, luscious blonde hair
and a mouth that looks like
angels would consider straying
to the dark side for one taste.
The Viking Gods were kind to
our girl last night.

BLUE

Okay, I'm on board.

COLLINS

fans self

HONEY

Why do you guys get all the
good ones?? WHERE IS A MAN
TO PLUNDER MY
THIGHS??????

COLLINS

As a woman who has abstained for YEARS I need details. Dirty, filthy details. GIVE THEM TO US Ella! HURRY!!!

I chuckled, typing out a quick reply I knew would enrage my friends.

ELLA

A woman never kisses and tells
;)

ANIKA

YOU BITCH!!!

COLLINS

You do you, hun. But seriously, how big are we talking? <------------8 ???

BLUE

Just wait until Monday. We WILL get all the tea!

HONEY

WHY ARE YOU DOING THIS TO US???????? Meanie!

Smiling, I locked my screen, sparing a final glance in the bathroom mirror.

"Okay, you're good Now get to work."

I wasn't due at the restaurant until early afternoon, but an owner's work was never done. I pulled out my laptop, setting it up on the kitchen island. I stood in the doorway of my pantry, contemplating breakfast options when I heard my front door open.

My heart skipped.

"Hello?" I called, stepping away from the pantry.

"Hey, you're up." Gunnar rounded the corner, carrying a large takeout bag and two coffee cups. "Sorry it took me so long. Anika wanted to make you something special. Said something about—" he continued to speak while placing items on the counter beside my laptop.

He'd changed. The damp clothes that I'd thrown in the dryer last night were gone, replaced with a shirt and dark board shorts. He smelled fresh, a mix of soap, salt, and him. I watched as he pulled a backpack off one shoulder, dropping it on the floor.

"Hope you don't mind. I brought an overnight bag. No big deal if you're not comfortable—"

My body reacted before my mind caught up. I launched myself at him, wrapping myself around him like a koala. I pulled his head down, pressing frantic, open-mouthed kisses to every part of skin I could reach.

His hands slipped down, palming my ass before boosting me up. My legs wrapped around his hips as we kissed, our tongues tangling in a desperate gasping slide. He twisted, shifting so I sa on the island counter, his cock now perfectly level with my pussy.

I pulled back, urgently tugging at the drawstring of his shorts. Desperately I shoved them down, reaching to grasp his cock. His thick length landed in my hand—hot, hard, and already pulsing with need for me.

Me.

I groaned, shifting so I could guide him to me.

"Stop. Condom," Gunnar groaned out as I rubbed the head of his cock against my clit. My wetness coated him, both of us throwing our heads back in a simultaneous moan.

"Pill," I panted, unwilling and unable to halt the desire pulsing through my bloodstream. "I'm on the pill. Please, can you just—" I pulled him to my entrance, tilting my pelvis toward him. "Please—"

"I'm clear, but pregnancy chances and—"

"In me," I demanded. "Now"

Gunnar slammed home, our bodies locking.

"Fuck," he bit out, thrusting again. "So good. So. Fucking. Good."

He pounded me on my breakfast bar, ripping my top down until my dress fell below my breasts. Cupping my breasts he lifted them to his hungry mouth, laving them with attention.

"I'm gonna—" my breath caught, my body tensing as I danced on the edge of an orgasm.

"Now," Gunnar ordered, thrusting hard. "Come for me, Ella." He dropped a hand, pressing a finger against my clit.

I screamed, dying a million little deaths as pleasure overrode all other senses. The waves of clutching, delicious tension flowed through my body as I milked his cock. Distantly, I felt his cum, his heat adding to my enjoyment.

Gunnar held me tight, one hand lazily stroking my hair as I returned to myself. I pulled back a little and looked up to find him smiling.

"Good morning." Satisfaction glinted in his eyes. "Miss me?"

I took one look at his beautiful face—a face that had quickly become so dear to me—and burst into tears.

"Hey, hey. Shit!" He lifted my chin, pressing a kiss to my forehead. "What's all this? Did I hurt you?"

I'd been so convinced he'd left me—that this connection had been one-sided. Horrified by my reaction, I ducked my head, shifting to try to escape him.

He cupped my cheeks, holding me in place as he searched my face. "Ella, baby. Talk to me."

"I thought you'd gone," I admitted, watching confusion cross his face. "You didn't leave a note."

He blinked. "After last night, you thought I'd just—leave?"

I shrugged, feeling suddenly vulnerable. I leaned away from him, pulling the straps of my dress up, covering my breasts. "I don't really know you, Gunnar. You could have been the type to wham, bam, thank you, ma'am."

He sighed. "True, we've been moving fast. Can't say I'm sorry, though." He stepped back, laying a hand on my thigh as he gave me a little space. "Ella, you're amazing. This thing between us—it's—special. Unique. I'm not leaving. And if I was, I'd make damn sure to let you know where I was going." He pulled me into his chest, holding me close. "I'm sorry I upset you."

I let him hold me, fighting to bring my emotions under control.

"Sorry." I scrubbed at my face, giving him a

watery smile. "I just—you're right. What we have is different. I've never had this reaction to someone before."

"I know, baby."

He pulled me back to him and I revelled in the feel of his strong arms holding me tight.

"Come on," he whispered. "Let's eat."

CHAPTER 6

"**H**ere she is! The queen of the hour!" Anika stood from her seat beginning a slow clap as I walked across the restaurant floor. "Strut queen! Strut!"

Laughing as Collins, Honey, and Blue joined her in a standing ovation—knowing I had no other choice but to let them have their fun—I brazened it out, lifting my arms above my head and sashaying my way over to them.

"Spin, girl! Spin!"

Rolling my eyes, I did a little twirl, laughing when Honey let out an earsplitting wolf whistle.

A few years back, Anika and I had joined a local book club. Within two meetings we'd figured out that we were in the completely wrong group for us when Anika's pick—a steamy bad boy billionaire romp—had resulted in the club instituting a blanket ban on romance novels. Despite our protests, the older couple who had led the club insisted that anything containing more than one sex scene would not be considered appropriate reading material.

In an act of rebellion, Anika had stormed out, leading Honey, Collins, Blue, and myself to what she termed 'the promised land'—all the romance books we could ever want. And so began Steamy Book Club—every two weeks on a Monday we met over books, booze, and burgers at the closed Bronze Horseman.

Honey, a chubby blonde with a big heart and sunny disposition often wore character-themed outfits, and today was no exception. Dressed in a ballgown—a nod to the Queen in the book we were currently reading—she looked like a regal princess, the crown on her head wobbling precariously. In contrast, Anika in her regular jeans and light shirt looked almost shabby. Predictably, her book lay on the table in front of her neatly tabbed and ready for discussion.

Rounding out our party of five were Collins, a yoga instructor and physical therapist who worked at Honey's clinic, and Blue, who worked as a nurse in town. Collins wore a green sun dress that complemented her pale skin and dark hair, bringing out the rich emerald of her eyes. Blue wore a hot pink jumpsuit, her tumble of dark hair left to flow wildly about her shoulders—hinting at her cheeky personality.

"So," Collins said, the first to retake her seat at the table. "Tell us *everything*."

I sighed, pulling my book from my tote and dropping it on the table. "Why do I have a feeling we're not going to talk about this magnificent novel today?"

"Because one of us finally has a real-life love story to dissect?" Honey answered, poking her tongue at me. "Come on, spill the beans!"

"What is there to say?" I asked, taking a seat at the table. "Gunnar is—"

"Okay, his name is Gunnar." Blue leaned forward, her dark eyes flashing with amusement. "Do you know his surname?"

"Larsson."

"Should we google him?" Collins asked. "Just to be sure?"

"Already on it." Anika held up her phone, typing furiously as she searched for info.

"Guys! Come on, this is a complete overreaction." I reached for her cell, groaning when she twisted away, holding it out of my reach.

"We're overly protective; sue us." She continued to tap her screen, her fingers a blur. "Oh, I got him!"

While I might have protested their heavy-handedness, I couldn't deny wanting to know a little more about the man I'd welcomed into my home.

"Let's see." Anika scrolled down the screen. "He co-owns a shipbuilding company with his brother. They specialise in fishing and recreation vessels. Looks like an inherited business but a successful one." She glanced up, her expression mildly approving. "I didn't pick him for a rich kid so kudos to him for not being a jerk."

"What else?" Honey asked, rapidly taking notes. "Do we need to order a background check?"

"You guys!" I shook my head, laughing when Collins handed me a beer.

"You better drink deep," she encouraged with a wink. "We're gonna be snooping for a while."

In the space of a half-hour, they'd managed

to uncover an ex-girlfriend, three social media accounts, and a photo of him in a swimsuit from college.

"The man," Blue murmured as she enlarged the photo, zooming in on his groin area. "Is packing heat."

I flushed, shaking my head. "I cannot believe we're objectifying him. Isn't this what we've been fighting against for the last few centuries?"

"I can be a feminist and a perve," Collins said dryly, accepting the phone from Blue. "The two are not mutually exclusive."

Laughing helplessly, I turned to Anika for support. "Please tell me we're going to move on from this subject soon?"

"Nope." She crossed her arms over her chest, staring at me with a Cheshire Cat grin. "You like this guy."

Damn.

"Yeah," I admitted. "It's gone a little beyond infatuation and attraction now."

"Already?" Honey asked, her tone sceptical. "Not that I'm saying you can't fall in love immediately, but what have you guys done besides—" she made a jerking motion with her hand.

"Ladies, the man has not left her side since

he arrived." Anika pointed at the bar behind us. "He sits in that chair watching her work. He follows her like a lost little duck when she goes to take out the trash. He ate all her breaks with her and then followed her home—no doubt to ravish our girl's body." She cocked an eyebrow. "Am I right, Ella?"

The heat in my cheeks could have rivalled the sun. "Yes."

"Oh." Collins pressed a hand to her chest. "He sounds lovely."

"Obsessed with her." Anika stabbed a finger in my direction. "And it's about damn time too. Our girl deserves nothing but the best and this guy?" She waggled her finger knowingly. "He's a good one."

I shook my head. "You guys are acting like we're about to get married. We're not. It's not even on the cards."

"You sure? Cause every time I see you two together...." Anika growled.

"Sex," I pointed out. "Does not a relationship make."

"But let's be honest." Blue tipped her bottle toward me. "You're not a one-and-done kind of girl. If you were, you'd have done the deed years ago."

"That's a great point." Honey tilted her

head to one side, the crown on her head barely hanging on. "What was it about this guy that got your juices flowing?"

I looked down at my hands, trying to find the words I needed to explain the craziness of the last few days.

"He looked at me with desire. He looked at me how I've always wanted a man to look at me." I pressed a hand to my belly, trying to calm the butterflies that had taken flight. "He made me feel seen."

Honey sighed dreamily, propping her chin on her hand. "Does he have a brother?"

"Two, actually."

"I'll take them."

I snorted at her offer. "You wouldn't know how to handle two men. Blue on the other hand...."

Blue tossed a pen my way, groaning. "Stop it! You know nothing ever happened between me and the Double Ds."

"But you want it to." Collins cocked an eyebrow. "Admit it."

"Maybe, a long time ago." She waved her hands dismissively. "But that's all water under the bridge now. They're back and they haven't bothered to even say hi. I'm fine with moving on with my life as well."

"Hmm, definitely sounds like it." Anika rolled her eyes. "You all give far too much power to men. You should be more like me."

"A hoe?" Collins teased.

"A slutty-mc-slut-slut," Anika agreed proudly. "Using and discarding men once you're done with them. No one needs the baggage they bring."

A beeping sound floated from the kitchen.

"And that'll be lunch. Be right back."

I watched Anika leave, wondering if I could ever be as cavalier as her about sex.

"Ella?"

I focused on Collins.

"Go balls to the wall. Don't take for granted what you've got." She sucked in a breath, pain flicking across her face before she shuttered it. "If you want him, go for it."

Blue squeezed Collins' hand. "You okay?"

She nodded. "This is about Ella, not me." Collins swiped at a stray tear. "Can we refocus on her, please? Or change the subject?"

Honey—always the one to lighten the mood —lifted her book. "Can we talk about the hero's dick piercing? I did *not* see that coming."

A bang echoed in the kitchen.

"The dick piercing!" Anika yelled, poking her head out the pass window. "That motherfucking dick piercing! I nearly came reading that scene. What in the actual *hotness* of all that is sexy was that?"

Grateful to be surrounded by women who loved me and wanted the best for me, I resolved to consider their advice.

But for now? Dick piercings.

CHAPTER 7

"This is gorgeous." Gunnar spread his arms out wide, taking a deep breath of the salty air. "You don't get places like this back home."

The Bronze Horseman was closed on Mondays and Tuesdays, and apart from book club yesterday, I'd spent all my free time with Gunnar.

Not a hardship.

With the weather so perfect, I'd decided to show him the Cove's secret beach. While it necessitated a long trek through the national park and down into a cave, exiting onto the pristine beach with it's beautiful rock walls and perfectly white sand made the walk worth it. In the decades I'd been coming here I'd only ever once found it in use by another local.

I reclined on my beach towel, adjusting my glasses against the sun's glare. "What is Cape Hardgrave like?"

Gunnar dropped to the towel beside mine.

"Our coastline isn't anywhere near this dramatic. It's mostly long stretches of white sand with giant piers stretching out to the deeper water." He covered his eyes with his arm as he stretched out, tilting his head back to enjoy the sun. "And there are always tourists— even in the middle of winter."

I tried to picture him leaving that bustling area for the relaxed pace of the Cove.

"Sounds busy."

He chuckled. "Understatement. The place is a mecca of activity." He peeked at me from beneath his arm. "I'd forgotten what quiet felt like."

Sand swirled as I created patterns with my fingers, considering his statement. "You like being busy?"

It wasn't a question so much as a statement.

"Mm." His foot stretched to touch mine. "This is the first break I've had in years."

"Why years?"

He shrugged. "The business needs me, you know how it is."

I frowned. "Not really. Anika and I make a point of taking a holiday every year. We want to ensure that we have longevity, and killing ourselves over our restaurant isn't going to achieve that."

Gunnar lifted his arm, opening one eye to blink at me. "Every year?"

I nodded.

"Huh." He rolled to his side, propping his head on his arm. "Would you ever consider heading my way?"

I swallowed. "I guess that depends."

"On?"

I stared down at my fingers, watching the patterns form in the sand. "You said it's quite a busy place."

"It is."

I glanced up but found myself unable to hold his eyes. "I might have some trouble finding a place to stay."

He sat up. "Ella. Are you asking if I'd put you up?"

I shrugged.

"Baby." He shuffled forward to lay hands on my knees. "Ella, look at me."

I forced myself to meet his gaze.

"Why on earth would you think you're not welcome?"

I shrugged.

He shook his head. "Is this a fling for you?"

I bit my lip, unsure of how to answer. "Is it for you?"

"Fuck no." He combed his fingers through my hair, his gaze direct. "You're incredible, Ella Bronze. And while this might have started fast, I'm not just hanging around for the sex— though it's a nice bonus."

He paused, seeming to search for the words he needed.

"You intrigue me. You're a boss woman— stern and direct, ambitious and motivated. You light up when you talk about your work and I adore that." He brushed sand from my shoulder. "But you're not like me. You don't live and die by the turn of the clock. You're not thinking about work every minute of every day. You're not consumed by your ambitions. And I find that...." He trailed off.

"You find that?" I prompted.

"Intriguing. You push me to see things differently. You're challenging me in a way I haven't been before." He ran a sandy hand through his hair, the damp strands catching the grains. "I'm not sure what to make of you if I'm honest. I can't find the box you fit into."

"I need to fit into a box?"

His hands dropped to my legs, gliding down their length. "It'd make my life a whole lot easier."

"Why?"

He chuckled, tracing the lightning tattoo on my ankle. "Just trust me." His thumb grazed my tattoo for a third time. "Tell me about this."

"My tattoo?"

"Mm. What's it mean?"

I watched his fingers slowly follow the zig-zag pattern on my skin.

"I want to be proud of the body I'm in. There are many times in life when I've looked in a mirror and found myself wanting. This—" I tapped the tattoo. "Reminds me to love my thunder."

Gunnar leaned down to kiss the ink. "You're gorgeous, Ella. This world will put you down—even when you've done nothing wrong. I'm glad you're not listening to it."

I tilted my head to one side. "That sounded like you speaking from experience."

He huffed. "That's because I am. Sometimes, no matter how hard you work or how much you fight, people will still crap on you."

I winced. "I'm sorry."

"Thanks, but it was a long time ago."

"Doesn't make it any less painful." I hesitated. "Do you want to talk about it?"

"No." His lips quirked. "But I will because you asked."

He looked off to the distance, his gaze unfocused. "Dad had a heart attack. Only minor—thank the Gods. But it put him out of commission for a while. I took over and—" he grimaced. "I botched a job. Badly. I'd been distracted, worried, but it wasn't an excuse. People got hurt and it damaged our reputation." He sighed. "It took us years to regain the clients we'd lost."

"Is that why you work so hard?" I asked. "Because you feel guilty?"

"Not guilt. Responsibility. Our employees rely on me for their livelihood. They depend on me to ensure they have a job and can provide for their families."

"That's a big weight to take on."

He shrugged. "Is it any less than you do?"

A wry smile touched my lips. "Touché."

He seemed to shake off the morose mood that had descended.

"Come on." He rose to his feet, pulling me up with him.

"Where?" I asked, laughing when he bent to throw me over his shoulder. "Gunnar! Put me down! I'm too heavy."

"Nonsense." He headed for the water. "You ever make love in the ocean?"

Squealing, laughing, and soon begging—the man claimed another one of my firsts.

CHAPTER 8

Gunnar

The days blurred while I remained in Ella's town. I didn't spend all my time with her, despite my best efforts. I ordered parts for the yacht and did general maintenance. I checked out the town, impressed by the number of tourists I saw floating about while remaining confused by the lack of local attractions available to take their money.

The Cove seemed to be a strange mix of local creative stores selling their small goods, and hardened fishermen salty as the sea. Sandwiched between two bigger cities, the town sat smack dab in the middle of some of the prettiest coast I'd ever seen. Considering the proximity to the cities, and the increasing tourist dollars, Ella's idea of expanding her offerings wasn't a bad one.

"Hey," Ella called, waving from the dock. She held up a paper bag. "I brought dinner."

I wiped my hands on a rag, drinking her in. "Get that gorgeous ass over here."

She laughed, sashaying down to my mooring. "Permission to come aboard, Captain?"

"Only if you pay the charge."

She giggled, springing across the small gap to the stern and rising on tip-toe as I pulled her close, greeting her with a long, slow kiss.

"Hi," she whispered, pulling back.

"Hey, baby." I pressed my forehead to hers, palming her full ass.

Fuck, I loved her curves. Full, lush and perfectly decadent, her body reminded me of a dessert buffet. From the taste of her cherry lips to the cream of her cunt, anytime she was around, I wanted to lick her from top to bottom, making her squeal and sigh in equal measure.

"Good day?"

"Better now." Her grin slipped, a small frown marring her forehead. She pulled away, busying herself with our dinner.

I knew Ella well enough by now to understand she wanted to ask something but feared the answer. And I knew exactly what question she was avoiding asking—it was the same one I'd avoided answering for the last week.

As if hearing my thoughts, my mobile rang, my brother's ringtone—the Funeral March—carrying over the breeze. In the distance, a storm rumbled across the ocean, promising a deluge later that night.

Ella laughed. "You better answer that."

I gave a long-suffering huff, pulling the phone free and sliding my finger across the screen to answer. "Brother."

"When are you coming home?" Erik sounded annoyed.

First you ask me to take a holiday. Now you want me back?

"Soon," I replied, my answer as vague as it had been every other time he'd asked.

"Gunnar, I need a date. I know I told you to take a break, but this is getting ridiculous. We've got clients waiting to place orders and guys pulling overtime to cover your work. Not to mention we need that yacht back here at some point. You were meant to be back two weeks ago."

"I got held up. That part—"

"Arrived last week. I know because I just paid the fucking invoice. What the hell is going on? Are you dying? Shit, do I need to call Ma?"

I watched Ella from across the deck. She'd settled on one of the chairs I'd set up for evenings like this. Tipping her face to the waning sun, her eyes closed, a small smile playing at the corner of her mouth.

"Ella," I finally admitted. "It's Ella."

"The girl you met?"

"Mmm." I turned away, keeping my voice low. "I need a favor."

"Does this include extending your vacay cause the answer is no?"

"I'll come back," I promised. "If you do this, I'll be back next week."

"Why do I feel like I might regret this?"

I glanced over my shoulder, offering Ella a smile. "I'm going to ask Ella to move to Cape Hardgrave. Can you check out that warehouse next to The Literary Academy? It'd be perfect for—"

"Are you shitting me right now?" My brother interrupted. "You've known this girl all of—what? Two weeks? And you're talking about moving her to the Cape, and getting her to do what exactly?"

"If we buy the warehouse next to Nan's bookstore, Ella could set up another arm of her restaurant."

"And you've spoken to her about this?"

I cleared my throat. "Not just yet."

"Gunnar...."

I could practically feel the waves of frustrated displeasure rolling down the phone lines.

"Trust me, Erik. She's gonna say yes."

He sighed. "You love this girl?"

I grunted. I hadn't told her yet, was planning some perfect moment when I revealed all—my plans for her restaurant, my love for her, the fact I'd already started searching for a house for us back in the Cape.

"I'd like it noted I think this is a terrible idea but I'll do what you ask."

"And," I said, knowing I was about to push my luck. "I might need you to come down and help me move her stuff."

After a silent beat, I pulled the phone away from my ear, checking the connection.

"Erik? You still there?"

"I'm driving down tomorrow."

"What?"

"I said, I'm driving down tomorrow. We'll spend the weekend in God only knows where and work out if you're being blinded by good pussy, have suffered a head injury, or if this is one of those kismet things Ma's always trying to convince us of."

I ignored the pussy comment. "It's not a head injury."

Erik chuckled. "Brother, I'll be the judge of that."

"Shit." I ran a hand through my hair. "You sure you need to come?"

"Gunnar, I've never known you to go gaga over a woman. This girl must be pretty fucking special for you to not only extend your vacation but be contemplating moving her in with you." He sighed.

"I may be your business partner, but I'm also your brother. Family comes first. You want this girl, you want to make it work. I'll go balls to the wall to help you however I can. You know that."

I did. My family was the best part of my life, and I knew they'd adore Ella.

"Let me check with Ella. Normally I'd say book your own hotel, but I have a feeling she'll want to put you up."

I didn't mention that the one motel in town looked like it had seen a murder or two.

"As long as I don't hear you doing the nasty, I'll stay where I'm put."

I thought back to last night's activities. I'd tied Ella up, binding her hands and wrapping rope around her body in intricate knots, drawing out her orgasm, teasing her until she screamed through her release.

The Japanese called it Shibari; I called it spank bank material.

"Bring earplugs," I told him, not even caring when he groaned complaints down the line.

"Fine. I'll see your ugly mug tomorrow." With that, he hung up.

I tucked the phone into my back pocket, turning slowly back to Ella. She'd pulled a big floppy hat from her bag, shading her delicate skin from the sun.

"All good?" she asked.

"Yeah, babe." I parked my ass in the chair across from her, enjoying the view. "My brother, Erik, he'll be coming to town tomorrow to stay the weekend. You cool with that?"

Her body tensed, but she kept her voice casual. "Is he coming to help you with the boat?"

I hesitated.

Erik hadn't been wrong. The part had come in last week, and it had taken me less than a day to fix it. I just hadn't expected to meet Ella.

Now or never.

"The yacht's fixed," I finally admitted, watching carefully for her reaction.

"Oh." She played with the skirt of her dress. "Does that mean you're heading home?"

Not without you.

"Not yet." I reached across, linking our fingers together. It was time I laid it all out there. "We've got a great thing going here. I want to keep this going."

Her cheeks coloured. "I know—I do too."

I grinned. "Good. My brother's gonna come down and stay for the weekend to meet you."

"Meet me?"

"Yep." I leaned in, pinning her with a look. "Ella, you gotta know. This isn't temporary for me. This keeps going the way we've started; it'll get to a point pretty quick where I want to marry you."

She sucked in a breath, looking overwhelmed. "But—" she trailed off, blinking frantically. "What about your business?"

I grinned. "I've got it all sorted. How do you feel about—"

"Wait, I need to say something." She smoothed down her skirt. "Gunnar, I just want you to know—you don't owe me anything. If you get home and this turns out to be—to be—" She swallowed. If this turns out to be nothing more than a summer fling, then that's okay. I'll be okay. You don't owe me anything."

Oh, no. No fucking way was I letting her think this wasn't anything more than a casual fuck. I thought our talk at the beach had made clear my intentions. I guess I was wrong.

"Obviously, I need to step up my game." I surged to my feet, pulling her up with me. Tugging her behind me, I led her to the cabin and assisted her down the stairs. She followed like an innocent lamb to the slaughter.

"This is...." Ella said, trying and failing to suppress a smile. "Pretty awful."

Dated and in need of a major overhaul both in terms of décor and machinery, the owner of the yacht had picked it up for a song and was willing to pay for the work.

It had a full kitchen, bathroom, seating area, and a bedroom tacked onto the back. That's where I took her, pulling Ella through the small cabin and into the tiny room. With its psychedelic panelling and black roof, the small cabin reminded me of a horror house at the carnival.

Good thing my cock didn't give a shit about décor.

I crowded Ella onto the bed, tossing her skirts up and diving for her underwear.

"Gunnar!" she gasped, trying to squirm away. "Wait."

"No," I grunted, hooking two fingers into

her underwear and tearing them down her legs. "I need to taste you, baby. Need to show you, you're mine."

She gave in, letting me pull her clothes off, then spread her thighs. I kissed my way up the soft skin of her legs, placing delicate kisses on the inside of each knee.

"You're mine, Ella." I hovered over her core, watching the blush of desire tint her skin pink.

"You're my home. I want you to be where I am. I can no longer imagine living a life that doesn't involve waking up with you, breathing your scent, kissing your lips, laughing with you. And when I leave this earth, I'll find you, Valkyrie. I'll search all of Valhalla for you."

I glanced at her, echoing my words from the first night we'd spoken.

"Too corny?"

Her gorgeous gaze met mine, her eyes twinkling. "Absolutely."

I dropped my head, relishing in the taste of her cream. She blossomed under me, her body shuddering as her enthusiastic gasps and moans encouraged my efforts.

"Say you're mine, Ella." I hooked one finger into her, pressing against her g-spot. "You're mine."

Her body bowed up, lifting off the bed as she cried out in pleasure. "Gunnar!"

"Say it," I demanded roughly, my finger pressing in.

"I'm y-yours," she gasped out, begging for more, begging for release.

"Again," I barked, barely able to contain my need.

"I'm yours, Gunnar. I'm yours. You own me."

I pulled my finger free and surged forward, pulling her against my cock, impaling her with my hot length. We both gasped, our rhythm uneven, hurried, each straining for dominance.

It was hot, heavy, and unpracticed. It was some of the dirtiest, filthiest sex I'd ever had. I drove into her, growling praises as she panted my name over and over, my cock turning her into a mass of squirming, heaving need. Her breasts bounced with reckless abandon, and I reached a hand up, brutally cupping one while my mouth descended to suck on the other. She exploded around me, her hips thrusting against me, her pussy a tight vice of clenching pleasure milking my cock.

"Fuck," I roared, hips pistoning. Once, twice, I exploded, cum filling her insides, coating her with my scent.

I collapsed on top of her, rolling until I

was on my back, Ella draped across my front. She cuddled into my chest, our breaths equally rapid as we tried to find calm in the aftermath.

"That was—" She made a small purring sound.

I grinned, pressing a kiss to her forehead. "Fuck yeah, it was."

We snuggled together, the boat bopped gently under our bodies, lulling us into a meditative state.

"Are you sure?" she whispered into the quiet.

"Positive," I told her, not even needing to clarify.

She drew in a shuddering breath. "I want to take this plunge with you."

My arms flexed, holding her tight.

"I'm scared. No one has wanted me like you do."

"Their loss." I tilted her chin up, waiting for her to look me in the eye. I needed Ella to see how deadly serious I was. "You're beautiful, Ella. Every part of you. Your body, your soul. You treat everyone with sass and good humor. You strut your sexy ass around your home, and I go weak. I want nothing more than to see that smile on your face and kiss your lips. I don't have any doubts, baby. I haven't since the moment you guessed my beer. You're it for me."

Tears shimmered on her lashes. "I love you, Gunnar."

"I love you too, baby." I pressed a soft kiss to her lips. "Now, when do you want to leave? How much notice do you need to give Anika?"

She froze. "What?"

"I assume you'll need to find a replacement for yourself. It'll suck being without you for a period but I'll come down on weekends and—"

She sat up, her hair falling over her chest. "What are you talking about?"

Something in her tone sounded off.

"Moving to Cape Hardgrave. What do you think I'm talking about?"

She stared at me, her mouth forming a small o.

I reached for her, not liking the space between us. "Baby, what—?"

She pressed a hand into the middle of my chest, halting my movement. "Gunnar. Wait. Are you saying you want me to move with you to Cape Hardgrave?"

I nodded slowly, not liking her expression. "I've asked Erik to check over a few places for you. We could set up another restaurant in the Cape. The tourist traffic is good all year round and—"

"What makes you think I would ever leave Capricorn Cove?"

The hairs on the back of my neck rose, a prickle of unease settling in my chest. "I'm in the Cape."

"Yes, but my business is here."

"And mine is there."

She pressed her lips together, her cheeks flushed. "So you expect me to move but you're not willing to discuss this with me?"

"What is there to discuss? Capricorn Cove has nothing to offer. My business is established. You can move—"

"Stop." Icy rage filled her quiet order. "Stop now before I start to think less of you."

"Ella, please. This is—"

She rolled off the bed, reaching for her dress. "Stop, Gunnar. You're digging a hole you might not be able to come back from."

"I don't understand. What—"

Dress covering her nakedness, she whirled, stabbing a finger into my chest. "You're making decisions about *my* future. You're acting like an ass. My business, my house, my family, my friends, my *life* is here. Did it occur to you that every time I said I would never leave I meant it? Did it occur to you that I have responsibilities? Commitments? Dreams that revolve around this town?"

She shook her head, tears glinting on her lashes. "No. You just decided what was best for me without considering what was best for *us*. Have you looked around, Gunnar? Have you seen the rundown buildings and abandoned lots? Five years ago, our restaurant was that. Five years ago, Anika and I were hustling to make a go of it. Since we started our business money has come into this town. People opened stores. Artists began selling wares. Tourists stopped in and started spending money." She threw her arms out. "I did that. Anika and I did that. We're making a difference here. We're helping. And as much as I love what we're starting, you're expecting things of me I can't give."

Guilt and fear knotted in my stomach, a cold sweat breaking out across my skin.

"Ella, I'm sorry. Baby, please—" I reached for her, intending to pull her into my arms but her hand shot out, halting my move once again.

"Valkyrie, let me—"

"Shh." She frowned, tilting her head. "Can you hear—"

A siren wailed in the distance, growing stronger as more joined the call.

"Shit." Her face paled. "That's the emergency signal. We have to get to the rally point."

The sirens were as familiar to me as they would be to anyone who lived by the coast in Astipia.

"Where's the rally point?" I asked, reaching for my clothes.

She dropped down beside me, pulling on her own shoes as she answered. "At the community hall."

I nodded, tugging on my boots. "Ella?"

She glanced at me, one eyebrow raised.

"I'm sorry."

She nodded. "We'll discuss it later." She stood. "Now come on, we have to hurry."

CHAPTER 9

Gunnar

"A cruise ship has struck rocks off the coast off Carolina Island," the Chief of the volunteer coast guard, Roy, explained as around me people tugged on wet suits, zipped up life jackets and laced up thick boots. "It's a domestic cruiser—information is sketchy but it looks like it has about three thousand passengers and crew on board."

He checked his notes. "Ella, I want you to coordinate comms and the rescue center. Notify the hospital and have paramedics on standby. We'll need ambulances available."

My woman nodded as she took notes, her expression grim.

"I'll be in the lead boat, we need to assess

the situation before I clear anyone to get close. I expect, based on initial information, that we'll need tug boats and rescue ships. The wind and waves are high today thanks to an offshore swell. While that's working against us, I will say that we're lucky that the light should hold for a few more hours. That'll help get a few passengers to safety."

He paused, his gaze sweeping the room. "Be on the lookout for anyone who might be in the water—lifeboats may have been deployed. We'll update as we go. Coast guard is en route but they're at least two hours away. We're asking anyone who is willing to be on a rescue boat to get out there. With a ship this size, we can't do this alone." The older man checked his clipboard. "I'm going to deploy trained volunteers on each vessel. Listen to these people, they'll have comms back to Ella and to the coast guard."

He paused, his expression grim. "I want everyone to come back alive. This isn't the time to be a hero." He nodded once. "Okay, let's get out there. Good luck."

I dropped to lace up one of Ella's boots as she did the same with the other, desperate to talk to her. "You okay?"

She nodded. "I'm trained for this. I know

my role." Her gaze searched my face. "You're going to go out on one of the boats, aren't you?"

"I'm a volunteer back at home." I inclined my head toward the milling volunteers, their expressions determined as they took final orders from the Chief. "I'll follow the locals but I can't sit around doing nothing."

Someone called for Ella.

"Just a second." She cupped my cheeks, pressing a quick kiss to my lips. "Stay safe, okay?"

"You as well." I caught her hand, kissing her knuckles. "We've got a lot to talk about later. And I've got a lot to apologize for."

A shadow of a smile touched her lips. "Then you better come back to me, Viking."

With a final kiss she let me go, moving to the makeshift communications area.

"You volunteering?"

I glanced up to find Roy standing over me. "I am."

He eyed me up. "You military?"

"No, but I'm a trained volunteer coast guard back at home. I'm one of the group leaders."

"Where's home?"

"Cape Hardgrave."

"See much action?"

I shrugged. "We get our share. Nothing as big as a cruiser though."

He nodded. "Yeah, it's a hell of a day." He glanced down at his clipboard, making a note. "I'll put you on a crew with Collins and Honey. They're good women, experienced. You follow their orders, got me?"

"Yes, sir."

"They're readying boat five. You better hurry." He clapped me on the shoulder. "Gods speed, son."

I headed for the marina, easily finding boat five.

"You our third?" the curvy blonde woman asked, eyeing me up as she performed final checks.

"I am."

She gestured at herself, "I'm Honey. That's Collins." She nodded at the woman on the other side of the cockpit.

"Gunnar."

They both paused. "As in Ella's Gunnar?"

I nodded.

"Shit, small towns getting smaller." Honey reached under one of the seats to toss me a life vest. "Put this on. Helmets are over in the box."

I followed orders as they pulled away from the marina, jetting through the waves and out of the cove. Without the headlands to protect us, the wind whipped up the swell, the open water rough.

"How far?" I asked, crouched beside Collins as we readied blankets and life jackets.

"About forty-five minutes. If the coordinates they gave us are correct, we'll have to make it past Carolina's spit before we can see the ship."

We followed the other boats as they fought the big waves, the swell from a far-off storm pushing against us.

As we rounded the point of Carolina Island the extent of the damage became clear.

"Fuck." I raised my borrowed binoculars to get a better look. "Fuck."

Rocks had torn the port side of the hull open, no doubt flooding the engine room. The entire thing leaned heavily towards its starboard side, the waves threatening a complete capsizing.

The radio crackled, the Chief relying to Ella the extent of the damage.

"Urgent assistance required."

As we drew near, Honey throttled the engine, idling us closer.

"Where are the lifeboats?" Collins asked, her own binoculars lifted as she searched the water. "With this amount of damage they should be evacuating the ship."

"It's dinner time," I murmured, searching the seas on the opposite side for any sign of a wayward passenger. "Maybe they were in the dining rooms."

"If that's the case, this is about to get a lot more difficult." Honey grimaced as waves hit the cruiser, buffeting the wreck. "There's a decent chance she capsizes entirely."

We listened as the Chief relayed the situation back to HQ, Ella coordinating with the formal Coast Guard and Navy in the area.

The afternoon light quickly dwindled, the distance storm raging on as lightning occasionally lit the horizon.

Our orders came, directing us to where passengers assembled ready to climb down to our waiting boat.

"All right, we're a go." Honey maneuvered us closer, her expression grim. "Let's hope there's some—Fuck!"

A cluster of waves hit the cruiser, upsetting the ship's already precarious balance. We watched as slowly, horrifically, the cruiser tilted, capsizing in full and throwing passengers from the stern and into the water.

"Mayday, mayday, mayday!" The radio exploded with the call.

"Fuck, let's go."

Dodging rocks and waves, we hauled

children, women, and men out of the water, huddling them on the boat.

"We're full," Collins called, desperation in her voice. "We have to go back."

I wrapped an elderly woman in a thermal blanket. She gripped my arm, stopping me.

"But there are more in the water."

"I know, and we'll get them," I promised, laying a hand over hers. "But we have to be able to get you back to safety. We're already over capacity as it is."

Collins and I looked after the passengers, treating injuries and shock as Honey steered us back to the Cove.

"We'll need a refuel," Collins murmured as we prepared to dock at the marina. "They're gonna need us back out there."

I nodded grimly.

We worked quickly, unloading the passengers and handing them off to waiting emergency personnel. A quick refuel and out we went, rotating with boats coming back until the storm necessitated a cessation of all rescue activity, forcing us to do something no rescuer ever wanted.

We were forced to wait.

CHAPTER 10

Gunnar

"You know, when I said I was coming for the weekend I expected sun, surf, and sand," Erik complained as our boat roared across the open water and back out to the capsized vessel. "Not a rescue mission."

I elbowed my brother in the gut, shooting him a droll stare.

After talking to him on Thursday, he'd jumped the first plane to the nearest city and driven down to lend a hand. Between the news crews, Navy, coast guard, and emergency services—not to mention those we'd managed to rescue from the ship—the population of Capricorn Cove had tripled overnight.

Three days after it had first run into

trouble, the end of the rescue was beginning to come into sight. Of the three thousand people on the cruise ship, only the crew remained aboard. If all went well, everyone would be safe in the next few hours.

And, thanks to the cruisers quick-thinking Captain, if nothing happened between now and then, it would be the largest successful rescue operation in Astipia's history.

Ella's voice came over the radio, clear, strong, and reassuring as she relayed orders and coordinated with boats on the harbor.

"Your woman is a keeper," Erik murmured as Ella finished. "She knows how to keep her cool in a tough situation."

In the last seventy-two hours I'd managed to only steal minutes of Ella's time. Between transporting passengers, supporting refueling, and preventing media and tourists from approaching the wreck— not to mention her own duties as the coordinator—our free time had been minimal.

"She's incredible," I agreed.

Erik gave me a side-eye.

"What?"

He shrugged. "Just thinking."

"I know that look."

He chuckled. "The look that says, 'hey. I'm

an awesome guy capable of holding three babies at once'?"

My brother had made the news the night before after holding three screaming babies while their mother disembarked the boat. The photo of a grateful parent standing next to a laughing Erik had made international news this morning. And, according to our family chat, he had three fan pages set up in his honor.

"No, it's you're 'ask me what I'm thinking' look."

"I'm just thinking about you and Ella."

I narrowed my eyes. "What about me and Ella?"

He shrugged. "The woman is a keeper. But I don't see her leaving the Cove any time soon."

Didn't I know it.

I glanced away, rubbing a hand over my chest. "I'll convince her."

"All I'm saying is, maybe there are other options."

Movement caught my attention. Shielding my eyes from the ocean glare, I spotted a jet boat racing toward the capsized ship. "Hold that thought, I think we've got our first dickhead of the day."

Our job today was to provide backup in case the Navy and coast guard needed assistance to get the crew from the cruise ship back to the Cove. In addition, we were asked to prevent any sticky beakers from getting in the way of the rescue operation.

"I see him," Honey called from the cockpit. "You guys get ready for an intercept."

Our boat sped toward the disaster tourists, Collins lifting a megaphone to belt out a warning.

"This is a restricted area. If you stay in this zone, you will be fined."

The boat, crammed with young idiots, ignored us.

"Fuck I hate people." I glanced over my shoulder at Honey. "Bring her alongside, I'll see if I can reason with them."

"Good luck."

We drew alongside the vessel, forcing them to slow.

"You have to turn around."

The captain, a guy who I pegged as being in his mid-twenties, raised his middle finger, flicking us the bird.

"Oh man." Erik shook his head. "We're gonna have to call in the sworn guys, get them to deal with it."

I nodded. "Collins?"

"On it." She lifted the radio, calling it in.

"Hey, fuck you! This is a free space!" One

of the passengers lifted a can of beer. "Fuck
you!"

I dodged the first can. "Hey! Calm—"

The second can I saw a split second before
everything went black.

———

Ella

Anika smacked a paperback down in front
of me.

"Eat," she demanded, crossing her arms
over her chest. "Now."

I ignored my friend, narrowing my eyes at
the radio operator beside me. Maeve held up
her hands in surrender.

"Don't blame me, it was your boyfriend
that told her."

"And good thing he did." Anika tapped the
bag. "No food and minimal sleep? Ella, you
know better than this."

I sighed, rolling my eyes. "It's not as if I
haven't eaten this whole time. I ate lunch."

Beside me Maeve coughed, the traitor
revealing my deepest secrets. "Yesterday."

I could practically see the steam exploding
from Ani's ears.

"Yesterday?" she repeated. "Yesterday? Ella Renee Artemis Bronze, yesterday?"

Anika wasn't an official coast guard volunteer, instead volunteering as the president of the town's food bank. But during emergencies, you could always find her in our food van cranking out delicious, wholesome meals for anyone who needed them.

I sighed, knowing I wouldn't get any relief from my best friend.

"Maeve, you okay if I get a quick bite for a few minutes?"

"Half an hour," Anika ordered.

"Fine, half an hour."

She nodded, her stunning blue eyes dancing with amusement. "I'll be fine. We're only expecting the next transfers anyway. The real work won't start back up for another hour or so."

Discarding my headset, I allowed Anika to drag me from the makeshift control room and out into the sunshine.

"Gorgeous day." I tipped my face toward the sun.

"Sit." She stabbed a finger at a park bench. "Eat."

With a sigh, I sat, opening the paper bag to find a couscous and lamb salad, some flatbread, two pieces of fruit, and a cookie.

"You're the best."

"I am," she agreed, taking a seat beside me. "Now eat."

With a small sigh, I dug into my mountain of food, nearly moaning when the flavors hit my tongue. My stomach rumbled in appreciation, the poorly abused organ roaring to life.

We didn't speak until Anika was satisfied I'd eaten enough to be comfortable.

"So," she said, glancing at her wristwatch. "You still have five minutes before you're due back. Hit me with it."

I raised an eyebrow, my mouth full of cookie.

"The thing that's got you avoiding the man you're apparently shacked up with."

"Nothing."

"Ella." She crossed her arms, giving me a look. "I've known you since we were twelve years old and both faking a period to get out of swimming class. Tell me what's happening."

I sighed, wrapping up the remainder of my cookie. "Gunnar... did something."

"Do I need to kill him?"

I smiled. "No. But he was simultaneously an ass and giving me my wildest dreams. I don't know how to process it."

She glanced at her watch again. "You've got four minutes. Give me the cliff notes."

With as much abbreviated detail as I could muster, I explained Gunnar's misstep.

"So the guy wants you enough to move you across the country but not enough to have a conversation with you or recognize that you're also tied to your own town—did I get that?"

I chuckled. "Spot on."

She nodded. "I'd like to reiterate my initial position that one-night stands are preferable to relationships. You don't have to deal with any of this nonsense."

"Noted. I'll try to do better next time."

She reached out to muss my hair. "Don't sweat it, little friend. Be firm in your boundaries and clear in your communication. If it's meant to be, it will be."

"But what if I want it to be and he can't compromise?"

She sighed. "Then you'll have to. And as much as it pains me to say this—if he's the one you really want, noting I'm not sure you can really decide that in the short time you've been together, then I'll support you." She pulled me in for a hug. "You'll work it out."

I squeezed her tight, accepting the comfort she offered.

"I love you."

"I know." She sat back. "I'm too awesome not to love."

I laughed, giving her a shove. "And modest too."

"Ella?"

I straightened, stiffening at the Chief's call. My head twisted, spotting him striding toward us across the park. I rose, meeting him halfway.

"What's wrong?"

He shook his head. "Look, I don't know how to say this but... Gunnar's had an accident."

And just like that, the bottom fell out of my world.

———

I clutched Gunnar's hand as the paramedics rolled him down the corridor into the hospital.

"I'm fine," he grumbled. "This is nothing but an overreaction. Give me some painkillers and send me home."

"You got hit with a can and passed out. Your head is cracked open and you're bleeding, Gunnar. I'm not letting you leave here until you get an x-ray and stitches."

Out of the corner of my eye, I saw the paramedics exchange an amused glance.

"You should listen to your girlfriend," one of them advised. "She's right. Head injuries need to be taken seriously."

"I'd take it more seriously if I wasn't half-naked," Gunnar muttered, squinting against the bright lights in the hall.

"He's the one who stripped off. Said he didn't want to be covered in blood," Erik called from down the hall, trailing behind us. "I tried to stop him but it was no use. Apparently, he just had to be naked."

The stretcher rolled to a stop as one of the paramedics broke off, moving towards the nurse's station.

"Won't be long," the other told us cheerfully. "Jim's just checking you in. They'll get you settled in a room in a moment."

I continued to grip Gunnar's hand, needing the reassuring heat of his skin against mine.

"Ella?"

I glanced down at Gunnar.

"You should go back. They need you."

"You need me more," I snapped, soothing a gentle hand over his cheek. "There are other people who can help."

A slow smile crept across his face. "You still love me."

"I—"

"Ella?"

Grateful for the interruption, I turned, a relieved smile lifting my lips. "Blue! Thank the Gods."

Blue stopped in front of Gunnar's bed, her hands going to her hips. "I hear you've been in the war, young man."

Gunnar laughed then groaned, clutching his head. "Shit, don't make me laugh."

She tutted, gripping the end of the stretcher. "Let's get you to a room."

She took charge, easily steering us down a corridor as the paramedics briefed her on Gunnar's condition. In the small curtained space, they transferred him from the stretcher to a bed, wishing us luck before they left.

"Now," Blue tucked a stray chunk of her dark hair behind her ear. "Tell me what happened."

Erik answered, explaining the confrontation and Gunnar's injury.

Blue nodded, checking Gunnar's vitals. "Any vomiting?"

I listened as Erik answered her questions, stroking my thumb over Gunnar's hand.

"No. He passed out for twenty minutes. Lots of blood but seems in decent condition."

"Any confusion?"

Erik settled in the chair beside the bed. "He doesn't remember the first hour after the incident."

She nodded, making a note on her clipboard. "Any change in behavior?"

"A little aggression but it's settled now."

"I'm right here. I can speak for myself you know," Gunnar protested, as Blue shone a light in his squinting eyes. "It's just a headache and a tiny cut."

She snorted. "The doctor will confirm but it's looking like a concussion. You don't want to be like someone I know who thought it was 'just a tiny bump' and ended up with a horrible concussion for three months."

A memory popped into my head. "That was Drake, wasn't it?"

Blue shot me a surprised look. "You remember that?"

I chuckled. "Of course. He had to take all that time off school. You and Dane seemed like lost little lambs without him."

She blushed, her hair falling forward to cover her expression. "That was a long time ago."

"Your brothers?" Gunnar asked.

Blue shook her head. "No, they were foster kids my parents looked after until they aged out of the system. They're in the Navy now."

The privacy curtain snapped open, an older woman wearing a funky shirt and capri pants entered the small space.

"I'm Doctor Peg. Let's see what we're working with." She took the offered chart, listening intently as Blue explained Gunnar's situation.

With a brisk bedside manner, she checked him over, unwrapping the bandage from around his head, and making a little tutting sound when she examined the sliced skin.

"Let's run an MRI just to be sure there's no internal bleeding. I suspect not but I want to be sure before we send you home." She removed her gloves. "Blue, can you please organize a tetanus shot and painkillers—I'll make a note on his chart of the dosage—and clean the wound area. I'll staple it after the MRI."

She offered us a reassuring smile. "If the MRI comes back fine, we'll send you home tonight."

"And if it doesn't?" I asked, my gut twisting anxiously.

"We'll deal with that if it happens. Likely overnight observations at the very least but we'll see what the scans come back with."

I nodded, Gunnar's hand squeezing mine.

"We'll be right back with the shot." They both exited, drawing the curtain closed behind them.

"Hey," Gunnar said softly, drawing my attention to him. His eyes were still narrowed and his brow pinched as if he were trying to avoid the light. "I'm fine. It'll all be okay."

I drew in a shuddering breath. "I'm meant to be reassuring you."

"Yeah well, you can make it up to me with a sponge bath later."

"And that's my cue to leave." Erik stood, stretching. "I'll just go get a coffee or something. Ella, you want anything?"

I shook my head.

"I'll get you a donut just in case."

I chuckled, watching as he left. "Your brother is ridiculous."

"If you think that then I'm worried about what you'll think of the rest of my family."

I reached out to brush fingers across his brow. "I should call them, make sure they know you're okay."

He groaned, his eyes closing. "How about we wait for the MRI results first?"

"Gunnar... what happens if you go into a coma? I don't know all your medical history. Does Erik?"

"Fuck no. He's a great brother but barely remembers my birthday let alone medical shit." He sighed dramatically. "Fine, but don't call Liv. She's a nut and will freak out."

Gunnar had four younger siblings—Erik, Liv, Astrid, and Rune. While Eric shared the running of the shipbuilding business with Gunnar, the other siblings had branched out into their own careers. Liv was a television producer, Astrid was at college finishing a master's in Architecture, while Rune ran a bookstore.

"I'll call your mom. What's her number?"

He rattled it off as I pressed the digits into my mobile.

It was answered on the third ring. "Hello, Larsson residence; this is Jemma?"

"Mrs. Larsson?"

"Yes?"

I swallowed, feeling strangely nervous. "This is Ella. I'm here with Gunnar who's—"

"Oh, Ella! Hello! Please, call me Jemma. I've been dying to talk with you. How is my boy? Treating you well, I hope?"

I swallowed, making big eyes at Gunnar who rolled his then grimaced.

"Um, yeah he is. Only he's had an accident. He's a wake and functioning, just a laceration on his head that will require staples, and a suspected concussion. They're doing an MRI to double check there's nothing they've missed but they're positive at the moment."

A beat of silence followed.

"Ella?" Jemma's voice had changed, her tone serious.

"Yes?"

"Put Gunnar on, please."

I glanced at him. "Um, sure." I held the phone out to him. "Your Mom wants a word."

He sighed heavily, accepting the cell phone. "Hi Ma."

I could hear the shrieks from where I sat. Gunnar winced, pulling the phone away from his ear.

"Ma, calm down. It's not a big deal. No, I wasn't being an idiot. Some dick threw a beer can at me and I hit my head when I fell over. No, I wouldn't have *died*. Yes, I understand you want grandchildren. Yes, she's very nice. Yes, I love her. Yes, I've told her. No, I don't need you to come here. No, I'm fine."

He sighed heavily.

"Ma. Ma. Ma! Put Dad on."

My body warmed, a happy little fire crackling in my gut as his admission of loving me.

"Dad? Yeah, I'm fine. A bump to the head and a cut. Yep, couple of staples because of the location. Nah, we're fine. Ella's good." He shot me a smile. "Yep, Erik's here. Sure, I'll keep you posted. Thanks."

There was a pause then another eyeroll followed by an immediate grimace. "Love you too. Here's Ella."

He handed the phone back to me.

"Hello?"

"Ella, it's Sune. Thanks for taking care of our boy."

Gunnar's dad had the same booming voice as his son and I couldn't help but smile upon hearing it.

"Oh, no problem. He's easy to care for."

Gunnar reached out to entwine our fingers.

"Keep us posted. If you need anything let us know. He's got a thick head so I expect they'll send him home where he'll act like a man-child for at least a few days. Don't let him fool you with the poor-little-me act."

I grinned, already liking his parents. "I'll keep that in mind."

"Call us once you know more."

"Will do," I promised.

"Bye, Ella."

"Bye." I hung up, sliding the phone back into my pocket.

"Thanks," Gunnar sighed. "Sorry, they're nutty."

I lifted one shoulder in a half-shrug. "I don't know, they seem pretty normal to me."

He raised an eyebrow. "Normal? Shit, what do I have to expect from your family?"

"Oh, Viking." I raised up, leaning over the bed to press a kiss to his forehead. "I have four brothers. You can expect *all* the crazy."

CHAPTER 11

Gunnar

I woke to a headache, a dry mouth, and arms that were empty of Ella.

An unacceptable state of being.

With a groan I swung my legs over the bed, rubbing a hand across my face, grimacing as the late afternoon sun hit me right in the eyes.

"—and then he threw up. All over his date. It was spectacular."

My brother's voice floated down the hall, Ella's laughter tumbling after it.

What the...?

I pushed up, staggering a little as I attempted to shake off the sleep haze.

I'd been discharged from the hospital two

days before, and ordered to keep up the antibiotics and painkillers for another week. Despite my protests, Ella insisted I rest— mandating that I take an afternoon nap each day.

That it tended to end with a little afternoon delight was an added incentive.

Stumbling down the hall, my brain still a little foggy, I went in search of the woman who drove me crazy.

"So tell me about Gunnar at—"

"No," I interrupted, leaning against the door jamb. "I think Erik's told you quite enough already."

Ella and Erik's necks twisted, their expressions mirrors of amusement as they smiled at me from their place at the kitchen island.

"Welcome back to the world of the living." Erik pointed his beer bottle at me. "How are you feeling today?"

I scrubbed a hand over my face. "Did Ma ask you to check in on me?"

He snorted. "You need to ask? She expects a phone call and proof of life selfie if you want to prevent her from driving all night to get here."

I clapped him on the shoulder as I moved past him, headed for my girl.

"Hey, Valkyrie." I leaned down, capturing her lips in a gentle kiss.

She sighed, her body melting into mine, her weight a warm embrace against my aching muscles.

"Feeling better?" she asked, reaching a hand up to brush fingers against my forehead.

"Kiss me again and I'll tell you."

Behind us, Erik made a choking, gagging sound.

"Ignore him," I told Ella. "He doesn't appreciate romance or love."

"More like I don't appreciate cheap one-lines," Erik muttered.

"Says the man who used a one-liner in that bar in Tokyo."

Ella giggled as Erik snagged her hand, pulling her away from me. "You picked the wrong brother. I'm much smoother."

"Yeah, he is." I agreed, reaching out to flick his ear. "He waxes. Smooth as a baby all over."

Ella's gaze danced between us, her amusement clear. "Do I need to separate you two?"

"Only about fifty percent of the time." Erik gave me a once-over. "You're better today."

"I am." I ran a hand over the bandage, gratified that the site of my injury seemed less tender. "Just a bump. No biggie." I took a seat on the barstool beside my woman. "What have you been up to?"

Erik and Ella exchanged a glance.

"Well, the rescue has wrapped up," Erik answered, selecting a chip from the packet Ella had laid out. "Emergency services will be handing over to the salvage and recovery crews tonight."

"That's good." I reached for his beer, yelping when Ella slapped my hand.

"No alcohol until you get the okay." She handed me a glass of water. "Drink this."

"Spoilsport." I took the water with a sigh.

Erik watched us, his expression shuttered.

"What?" I asked him.

"You up for an excursion?"

I shrugged. "Probably."

"Nowhere too strenuous," Ella ordered, checking my bandage. We don't want a relapse."

Erik chuckled. "I was thinking we could check out the marina, but seeing Ella abuse you is also pretty fun."

I raised an eyebrow. "The marina?"

"Sure. See the sights, work out what this town has to offer."

I cocked an eyebrow. "Great coastline, a decent restaurant, and little else I think is the answer."

Ella snorted.

"Am I wrong?" I asked, genuinely interested in her answer.

"So wrong." She left the room only to return a few minutes later with a pile of boxes.

"Here." She dumped them on the counter. "Here are all the things Capricorn Cove has to offer."

I tugged the lid off one of the boxes to find a treasure trove of family photos, keepsakes, albums, and memorabilia.

"What is this?" I asked, lifting one of the photos to the light for a better look.

"My childhood, my history—the history of Capricorn Cove."

"You have skiing here?" Erik asked, flipping the photo so I could see a young Ella in her skis.

"Yep. The fields are an hour and a half outside of town." She rummaged in one of the boxes to pull a battered pamphlet free. "See?"

She spread it on the counter, showing us a map of the area.

To the south—of course—lay the ocean, the coastline a mix of swim beaches, protected coves, and rock pools. Islands dotted the area, each noted for its various fauna, flora, or landscape.

"There's a turtle recovery centre just inside the national park," she said, her finger tracing across the worn paper. "Capricorn Cove National Park—also known by its traditional name as Kominah National Park—has everything you could want for summer and winter. There's a campground, caves, hiking, and Lover's Lake which has an old lodge and cabins." Her finger followed one of the roads. "Outside of the park we have the agriculture areas—lots of farm-to-table options and a few wineries and microbreweries which are just starting up."

"And the skiing?" Erik asked, crowding closer.

"Over in the Juniper Ranges." She tapped the mountains to the east of the map. "Gorgeous year-round but especially so during ski season."

"You guys have a college here?" I asked, noting the icon on the map.

"Ravenburn College," Ella confirmed. "They specialize in marine and agriculture studies, literature and business." Her lips quirked. "See? We're not a completely useless town."

Our gazes met, hers shuttered, mine contrite.

"Ella, I owe you an apology."

"Oh, this ought to be good," Erik chortled.

I ignored my idiot brother, focusing on the woman I loved. "I made assumptions about this town before I really understood it. You were right. I shouldn't have assumed our only option was to move to the Cape. I shouldn't have made decisions for both of us."

"And he's sorry for being a pigheaded ass," Erik added. "And not asking you what you wanted."

"And for—that." I brushed my hand over her cheek. "I'm sorry, Ella."

"Thank you for your apology and for acknowledging your fault." The shuttered look in her eyes faded. "You're forgiven."

She glanced back down at the map. "But, you're also right. We have limited job offerings —the papermill, the remaining commercial fishing co-op, some emergency services, teaching, or a tourist job that may or may not pay anything." She blew out a breath. "Unless you're willing to invest in the town, the job offerings are slim. I just can't see how you'd be happy here."

"So, about that," Erik interrupted, tapping his fingers on the counter. "I may have an idea."

"Really?" I asked skeptically. "You?"

He flicked me the bird. "Yes, you fucker. I am capable of thought." He nodded at the map.

"Ella and you are both right. This town isn't capitalizing on the tourist market. Which is why I spoke to Rick."

I frowned. "Rick? Who's Rick?"

"He owns the marina," Ella answered, her expression thoughtful. "He's been trying to sell it for the last few years. Wants to move up to the main island where his grandkids live."

Erik nodded. "That's the one."

I scratched my chin. "You know, that isn't a bad idea."

Erik rolled his eyes. "Thanks for the crumbs from your table."

"It'd be a smart investment. You've got regulars and tourists. Give the marina an overhaul, add a few upgrades, target a few businesses to bring them in as a starter." My mind raced. "It's got merit."

"Not to mention," Erik added. "We could expand up here and capture trade from the northern islands."

Ella glanced from Erik to me and back. "I'm sorry, what's happening?"

"We've been talking about expanding the business," I answered.

"But real estate in the Cape is crazy expensive." Erik waved his hands around. "So why not here? As everyone keeps saying, this place could be a gold mine—if only someone invested in it."

Ella stared at me. "You could move your business here?"

I exchanged a look with Erik. "Maybe," I admitted. "We'd have to find workshop space and crunch the numbers but—"

"But it's possible," Erik agreed.

I watched a million emotions play across her face. "Ella, you okay?"

"You'd do all this? For me?" She looked overwhelmed, confused, disbelieving.

"Baby," I slipped off my chair to crouch between her thick thighs, my hands running up her silky skin. "I'd move the earth if you asked."

She shook her head slowly, her eyes glassy. "I didn't want you to turn your life upside down."

"Nothing's set in stone just yet," I reassured her. "But if I expected you to move to the Cape, I'd be a fucking hypocrite if I wasn't willing to do the same if there's a viable option."

She caught my face in her hand. "Thank you."

I grinned. "You can thank me later in be—"

"And that is more than I needed to know!" Erik burst in. "Shall we go check out this marina?"

I watched Ella, waiting for her answer. Slowly, she nodded.

"Great!" Erik slung an arm around her neck, giving her a squeeze. "And maybe we can get dinner at this little lady's restaurant?"

"You're paying," I warned him even as Ella waved me off.

"Family doesn't pay," Erik protested. "We're family right, Ella?"

"Of course, they do," I snapped, turning on my heel to head back to the bedroom to find a shirt. "Gotta support small businesses."

"Don't worry, you don't have to pay." I heard Ella reassure Erik.

"Yes, he does!"

Our argument continued until we got to the marina where, as the sun hung low in the sky, we walked every inch of the property.

"I mean, it's pretty horrible," Erik said as he poked at a rotting banister. "I can't see much that doesn't need to be replaced. Can't imagine the storefronts are much better."

We looked up to the row of stores that lined the boardwalk. They were included in the price and, apart from one selling bait and gear, stood empty.

"They've been vacant for as long as I can remember. I highly doubt they'll be fit for much."

"But if they were fixed up...." I trailed off.

"Fine." Erik tossed up his hands. "You've convinced me. We'll take it." He waggled a finger in my face. "But this is gonna be your baby. Don't come crying to me when you get splinters in your hands."

I grinned, holding out my hand for him to shake. "Promise."

CHAPTER 12

Gunnar

"Jesus Christ, slow the fuck down," Erik demanded from the truck's passenger seat. "The last thing we need is to fucking roll this thing."

I glanced at the dash, easing my foot off the gas as I registered my speed.

"It's been a month," I muttered. Erik sighed heavily beside me.

"Ah, young love." He shook his head. "Look, Ella's awesome, but you went decades without her. Surely you can live another twenty minutes."

Barely.

I didn't dignify him with a response. He'd get it one day.

I'd spent the last month closing out my responsibilities. I'd put my house up for sale, packed all my shit in a truck, and put a down payment on a home in Capricorn Cove.

Our house.

Ella hadn't been wrong about the older generation looking for a move. We'd been inundated with house offers when word had got around that she was looking to buy. She'd sent me pictures of one with two words—our home. I'd put a deposit on it that day.

I didn't care that it needed work or that we'd probably need to add additions at some point—the house sat up on a protected little block with views out to the ocean. The front of the massive block was flat, with plenty of space for a yard, entertainment, and even a shed. The back was a mess of trees and brush, but a sloping stair path led down to a private beach— complete with a small pier perfect for docking a little fishing boat.

We'd picked it up for a song and would be moving in this weekend. I had plans to fuck Ella in every room of the house. And that beach? Perfect for a little afternoon delight.

Beside me, Erik opened the manila folder, interrupting my daydream.

"We're gonna need to renegotiate this," he muttered for the umpteenth time since this trip started. "The terms are good, but I think we can do better."

I ignored my brother, focusing on navigating the tight turns that took us around the coastal road to home. We were in the final stage of negotiations to buy the marina—including the old fish market that would eventually become our new workshop.

"If we took that old yacht club and overhauled it, got Ella in to run it, we could make some serious buck with weddings and what-not," Erik muttered, making notes in the margin of a page.

My heart lifted as we turned the last corner, seeing the sign welcoming us to Capricorn Cove.

Home.

Ella.

I forced myself to slow the truck, abiding by the speed limit as I navigated to Ella's small cottage. We'd be picking up the keys to our new home tomorrow. Tonight was for our reunion.

I pulled in at a motel down the street from Ella's house.

"You know, maybe you should let me run this past Ella tonight. I think we could really—"

"Get the fuck out," I grunted, ignoring my brother's protests.

He sighed dramatically. "You really can't keep that girl to yourself. That's selfish."

I can today. Just watch me.

He slammed the door shut, calling through the window, "don't be late tomorrow. We need to—"

I drove off, bumping down the road, ignoring his yell. I hadn't held Ella in a month. A truly unacceptable occurrence.

I pulled the truck into her drive, noting with approval that her car sat ready—packed to the gills with stuff. Boxes sat on her porch, waiting to be loaded by the movers who were coming in the morning.

My truck skidded to a halt, gravel flying under the wheels as it protested. I parked, throwing open the door and quickly locking it, fumbling with the keys in my haste. I jumped the stairs to her porch, pausing to snatch the pinned note off the door.

I'm inside. Come find me.

I pushed through the door, throwing it shut behind me, and stalked down to her bedroom. Boxes lined each room as I passed, her frames and knickknacks, candles, and frills all packed away in preparation for the move. Only boxes and furniture too big to wrap remained, ready for tomorrow.

I found her in the bedroom. The room had

been stripped, empty except for the bed. No boxes, no comforts, just a bed still dressed in lavish pillows and white bedclothes. On it, in only a scrap of lace and a smile, lay my beautiful woman.

"Ella," I breathed her name as if it were air.

"Viking," she greeted, a naughty smile on her lips.

I stalked to the bed, hands coming to the hem of my shirt, jerking it over my head and tossing it heedlessly to the side. I paused at the foot, shoving down my pants and underwear, cock springing free as I closed the final distance to her.

My hands grazed her skin, her scent filling my nostrils as my mouth descended.

"Ella," I whispered as my lips touched hers. Our mouths met, hungry and desperate. Wet, hot, and hard, our tongues danced as we kissed, tasting that which we'd missed.

"Baby," I groaned, hands skimming down her sides. "I can't wait."

"Then don't," she replied, nipping playfully at my jaw.

I let out a feral growl. "Fuck."

Scooping her into my arms, I seared my lips to hers. Delicious heat spread rapidly throughout my body, pooling in my aching cock.

She tasted like home.

I pulled back, looking down at her exquisite body. "I like lace bras, but god damn if I'm gonna let you keep this one on."

I snatched her close, and once again, our tongues clashed, and lips grasped as my hands roamed her skin, touching and caressing, driving her passion higher. I suckled at her neck while edging the material down, revealing skin, tracing the curve of her breast through the lace.

I flicked her nipples with my thumbs, grinning as she gasped her pleasure.

"Oh!"

I watched Ella fight for control, her eyes glazed with passion, her lips plump and already swollen from our kisses. Ultimately, she gave up, surrendering to my pull as I easily unlatched her bra and drew it from her, tossing it across the room.

My mouth descended to suckle first one nipple, then the other while her hands gripped my head and her mouth panted words of encouragement.

"Please, Gunnar, please. Oh, please. Yes, like that! Please!"

I drew back. "Underwear off."

She helped me, lifting her ass to wretch them off, throwing the silky material away.

Once gone, she pulled me closer, hands reaching out to grasp my cock. She took me in hand, jerking slowly up and back, teasing my member.

"Jesus Christ, fuck. Fucking fuck, fuck," I groaned, fighting the urge to pump into her hands. "I've missed you, baby. Missed you so fucking much. Love you, Ella. Love you so fucking much."

I pressed kisses to her mouth, praising her, worshipping her as she fisted me.

"Can't wait," I panted. For the first time in my life, I was gonna lose control. "Need to be in you."

"Thank the Gods." She squirmed into position. "I've been dying for you."

I found her core, sliding fingers through her slick heat, finding her wet and ready.

"Baby," I groaned. "You're so fucking wet for me."

"I've been wet all day," she admitted, red flushing her cheeks. "It's been so hard not to—"

I surged in, both of us gasping as I filled her. Her tight pussy clenched around me like a vice, tight, hot, wet—fucking perfect.

I reached down, lifting her legs, encouraging her to wrap her thighs around me. I needed to be surrounded by her; I needed to glory in her.

We crashed together, two parts of one whole, our bodies meeting again and again in a brutal, glorious ritual.

"I love you!" she screamed as her body clenched, every part of her thrashing as she tipped over, falling into the chasm of ecstasy. I followed, emptying myself inside her body.

We collapsed, our bodies intertwined, our skin pressed tightly together.

"Don't ever leave again," she whispered, her legs and arms wrapped tightly around me.

"Never," I promised.

Our bodies cooled; the desire only slightly sated.

"Where's Erik?" she finally asked.

"At the motel. I didn't want him interrupting."

She giggled, her beautiful face lighting up. I pressed kisses to her cheeks, ignoring her squeals, enjoying the taste of happiness on her skin.

This is home.

Later, after more lovemaking and a failed attempt at showering that ended with the need for another shower, we headed to the Bronze Horseman in search of food.

In a booth, curled into one another, we ate slowly, discussing the next steps on our journey together.

"I don't expect it to take long," I told her, referring to the meeting Erik and I had tomorrow to finalize the sale contract for the marina.

"Well, the council is all for it. I've already been fielding calls from local builders eager to get their piece of any new construction." She chewed absently on a chip, a small frown furrowing her brows. "Actually, that's one thing you've never told me."

"'What's that?" I asked, tracing swirls across the delicate skin of her inner wrist.

"What your company is called."

"I haven't?"

She shook her head.

"And you never googled me?"

She laughed. "Of course not."

"I don't believe you."

She winked. "*I* never googled you. I never said others hadn't."

She picked up another chip. "But seriously, I don't remember us discussing it."

"It's Thor's Shipbuilding."

She jerked, a strangled sound coming from her throat. She coughed twice, the blockage clearing. I handed her a glass of water—urging her to breathe.

"You okay?" I half-rose, wondering if I'd need to perform a Heimlich maneuver.

"Yo-you-your company is called Thor's Shipbuilding?" Her voice sounded strangled.

I rubbed a hand over her back, frowning. "Yeah. Are you sure you don't need—"

She threw her head back, roaring with laughter. Heads swung our way, tourists and locals alike gaping at Ella as she lost all control.

"You-you-you're," she gasped, tears running down her face. "An ac-act-actual Viking!"

I shrugged, not seeing the humor in the situation. "I mean, I wouldn't say yes but—"

"Oh my God. I can't." She brushed away tears, beaming at me.

"Is this funny?"

"All my life, I've asked for a God to come and tame these thunder thighs." She slapped her beautiful legs, beaming at me. "And you arrived. This glorious Viking of a man, ready and willing to plunder my pussy. And best of all? You're a god of thunder. Thor's fucking Shipbuilding, if that isn't a sign, I don't know what is." She started laughing again, her joy contagious.

"Baby, you can call me whatever you want," I told her, pulling her close, one hand slipping under the table to cup her center in the dark. She froze, laughter dissipating as desire took over. "Just as long as you call me yours."

She rolled her eyes, groaning. "That's so corny."

"But true." I withdrew my hand, slipping it into my back pocket to pull a small pouch free. "I love you, Ella. I know we're just starting our lives together, but I want to do this right."

I handed her the velvet pouch, watching as she pulled the drawstrings open. Tipping the pouch into her palm, she gasped when a ring tumbled out. Princess cut white diamond surrounded a band decorated in Celtic knots with sapphires. She looked up at me, her eyes wide.

"Marry me."

Her beautiful eyes filled with tears even as her lips moved to deliver the answer I'd hoped for.

"Yes."

We kissed, me sliding the ring on her finger, her sobbing tears of joy.

"I'm so glad it was here," she whispered against my lips.

"This is the only place it could be. It's the first place I saw you." I nodded over at the bar. "I fell in love with a Valkyrie right there."

"And I, my Viking," she sniffed, grinning. "I love you, Gunnar."

"I love you, baby."

She tilted her face up, and I obliged her, willingly drowning in her kisses.

She called me her God of Thunder, but she was the one who'd summoned me—changing my world.

Corny? Hell yes.

Did I care? Not at all.

CHAPTER 13

Gunnar

"Oh look, it's Dane and Drake."

I glanced up from the cereal box I'd been perusing to see Ella pointing down the end of the aisle.

The men in question were tall and muscular. One broad, the other lean. Both had a look about them that said ex-military.

"Who are they?"

Ella rolled her eyes. "You remember, Blue's boys."

I wracked my brain trying to remember why that name sounded familiar. "The nurse who looked after me when I hit my head? The brunette?"

Ella nodded. "Yeah. She's sweet on them."

I eyed the men. "Both of them?"

"Uh-huh." Ella plucked the cereal from my hands, tossing it in our cart. "They're together but I think they want Blue to be with them too."

I pushed the cart, following Ella down the aisle. "And your town would be cool with that?"

She gave me a look. "I'm sorry, you're not?"

"Not what I meant." I raised one shoulder in a half-shrug. "Love is love, babe. I just meant this is a small town. Don't expect that people will be exactly welcoming of a polyamorous relationship."

Ella chuckled. "Then you haven't lived here long enough. For a while back in the sixties, there was a commune out in the mountains by Lover's Lake. Honestly, this town is all about love."

I reached over pulling her into me, pressing a kiss to her temple. "Mm, well it's certainly been that way for me."

She laughed, shoving me away, her engagement ring catching the light from the fluorescent bulbs above us.

A possessive kind of love warmed my blood.

"When we get home, we should—"

Ella cut me off, a hand flying to my mouth as she forced me back a step.

"What are you doing?" I asked against her palm.

"Shh! Blue's hugging Dane!"

I peered around the end of the aisle, catching sight of Blue hugging one of the two men.

"And?" I asked, completely baffled by my fiancé's behavior.

Ella tilted her head back, a small grin lighting her eyes. "And this could be the start of something wonderful. I don't want to interrupt her chance to be as happy as you and I are."

Well damn.

I leaned down, my arm hooking around her to pull her body against mine, our lips meeting in a hungry kiss.

I'm not sure how long we stood like that, our lips locked, our hands roaming each other's body.

"Ahem." A cough came from behind us.

We both twisted, an older gentleman with a cane and basket grinning at us.

"Sorry, kids." He nodded at the shelf behind us. "Normally I'd leave you alone but I'm in desperate need of pasta sauce."

Ella blushed as we moved out of his way.

"You two have a good day." He winked, moving off towards the registers.

Ella's head landed on my chest, her hair falling over her flushed cheeks. "That wasn't at all embarrassing."

"Lover's Lake commune, remember?"

She groaned. "Shudda up. Let's get this done then you can take me home and ravish me."

With pleasure.

EPILOGUE ONE

Ella

Dinner with a family of Vikings was... interesting. Due to Christmas being one of my busy seasons at the bar, Gunnar's family had volunteered to come to Capricorn Cove to celebrate.

I'd expected them to be a little rowdy—after all, I'd met each of them individually over the last few months and they'd each been joyous, friendly and loud, oh *so* loud.

And I loved it. I did. I loved that Gunnar's family were brash and bold, and embraced me wholeheartedly. They fully supported our relationship, and I adored them for it.

I just hadn't quite been prepared to experience them as a group. The Larsson's towered over me, bellowed over one another, and laughed uproariously with joy while toasting each other with legs of turkey, forks full of ham, and large mugs filled with my best beer.

As much as I joked about Gunnar being a Viking, tonight felt like a long house celebration, the family having returned from a successful raid.

Gunnar had settled me on the chair next to him, our thighs pressed tightly together, one arm slung over my shoulders as he laughed at something his sister said.

I smiled, basking in the joy that filled the room. Gunnar glanced at me, his grin still in place.

"All good, baby?"

"Mm." I raised my cup tipping it slightly towards him. "Should I bring the desserts out?"

He glanced at the table, chuckling at the ravaged remains. "Yeah, and I should probably tap another keg."

We'd shifted the festivities from our house, which was currently undergoing renovations, to the restaurant. Not only could it fit everyone, but it was only a short walk away from the motel where they were staying.

I pushed up, Gunnar following me. There was a flurry of movement as the family began to pile plates, collect cutlery, and head towards the kitchen.

"Oh, please don't!" I cried, gesturing at them to stop. "Sit! Please, we've got this."

"Many hands make light work, sis," called Gunnar's sister, Astrid, her arms full of a decimated platter of turkey bones.

I allowed them their moment then shooed them out of the kitchen, telling them to put on music, and help themselves to more beer. They didn't protest, leaving Gunnar and I alone in the kitchen.

"What can I help with?" he asked, rolling up his sleeves.

I tried and failed to ignore how that simple action changed him from simply sexy to every woman's wet dream.

"Ella?"

I jerked back, blinking. He watched me for a moment, a small, devilish grin creeping across his lips. His eyes darkened, heat burning in their depths. "You need something, Valkyrie?"

I opened my mouth then snapped it shut as a blush warmed my cheeks. "Your family is outside."

He took my hand, pulling me down the length of the kitchen and into the storage room at the back. Sliding the door closed, he shifted, backing me up until I pressed against a shelf containing bags of flour.

"You see something you like, baby?" His voice was low and gruff with desire.

I licked my lips, swallowing, acutely aware of the throbbing of my pulse and the heat of desire pooling in my lower abdomen.

"No," I lied. "Not when your family is just outside."

He tsked, that filthy grin still in place. "Liar, liar, your pussy's on fire. It wants me to touch it and make you feel good." His big hand slid down my side, wrapping around to squeeze my ass. "Admit it, baby. You want this."

I opened my mouth, to protest or to agree I wasn't yet sure, but instead, a needy little moan broke free, catching us both unaware.

Gunnar paused, his nostrils flaring before his control broke. He went for my mouth, devouring me with greedy neediness. I fell into him, letting him plunder my mouth.

His hands dipped, gripping my ass and boosting me up. I obliged, wrapping my legs around him. He pressed me back into the shelving, careful to ensure I didn't hurt myself. When he had me anchored, he shifted one hand, pushing my skirt up and running fingers between my thighs, finding my wet, aching core.

"Fuck." He broke off our kiss, his fingers gliding deliciously through the wet of my naked pussy. "Where the fuck are your underwear?"

I panted, each breath causing my nipples to graze against his chest. "This dress doesn't allow for underwear."

"You've been like this all night?"

"Yeah." I let out a little moan, my head falling back, eyes drifting shut as he played with my clit. "I thought you knew."

"Fuck." He circled my clit faster, working me in a way guaranteed to drive me crazy. "You're gonna get spanked for this later."

Can't wait.

His fingers disappeared and I whimpered, pressing myself forward. Between us, his hand fumbled at his crotch.

"It's okay, baby. Just gotta get this fly undone... there." His cock pressed to me, deliciously hard, hot and thick. "You ready, baby?"

I forced my eyes open, letting him see all my desire, all my need. "Always, Viking."

He thrust forward, burying himself to his hilt. We cried out, the friction and heat overwhelming. He pulled back, then thrust again, and my control broke. I no longer thought of his family waiting for dessert. I no longer worried about being interrupted or keeping quiet. I thought only of Gunnar, his smell, his feel, and his cock as it drove me higher, chasing my release.

"You like this, baby? You like knowing I couldn't wait to feel your pussy?" Gunnar muttered, thrusting harder. "You like knowing I'll be thinking about my cum dripping down your legs for the rest of the night? You like knowing I'm gonna fuck you on the table after everyone leaves?"

I nodded, heat wrapping around me, desire spiking. I dragged fingernails up his back, knowing that would drive him wild.

"You gonna come for me, Ella?"

"Yes," I groaned, feeling the pressure mount. "Yes, Gu—"

A strangled scream ripped from my throat. He fisted my hair, pulling me to him, merging our mouths together. Our tongues tangled as I milked his cock, feeling his hot release paint my insides.

Panting, we kissed. Our bodies were still hot with desire but the urgent need had been spent. My hands gently roved over his back, unable to keep myself from touching him.

"You okay?" He asked, pressing a kiss to my shoulder.

"Mm," I hummed. "I can't feel my legs."

He chuckled, stepping back and shifting to allow me to slide slowly down his body. I straightened my skirts, then reached up, fluffing my hair.

"How do I look?"

His smile was pure satisfaction. "Like you've just been fucked in the storeroom."

I sighed, flushing. "No helping it I guess."

He ran his thumb over the curve of my neck. "I love seeing my mark on you."

I groaned, covering my face with a hand as I pushed passed him. "Love bites aren't sexy, Gunnar. How many times do I have to tell you that?"

He chuckled, slapping me playfully on the butt as he followed me out.

We returned to the kitchen, snatching desserts from the cold room. Gunnar pressed a kiss to my lips, giving me a wink.

"Ready for round two?"

"I think I can handle it."

He pushed through the swinging door, both of us pulling up short—frozen in place by the chaotic scene before us.

Jemma gesticulated wildly at Gunnar's father as Sune yelled at Erik. Erik stood in front of a pair of police officers, staring down at a piece of paper, ignoring his parents. He looked like he'd been struck by lightning, his hair standing on end.

Off to the side, Astrid and Liv, and their youngest brother, Rune, were passing two screaming babies back and forth, each looking woefully out of their depth.

"What the fuck is going on here!?" Gunnar bellowed, cutting through the commotion. Even the two babies, who had definitely not been there before, quietened down.

"Sorry to be the bearer of bad news, Gunnar." Sheriff Tristan Rodriguez held up his hands in a helpless gesture. "We had these two kids dropped at the station today. No one saw the mother, she took off. Left one note though." He nodded at Erik who was still staring at the slip of paper. "The mother signed over responsibility to your brother."

I blinked, my gaze shooting to Erik, then to Gunnar.

"Excuse me?" Gunnar asked, setting down the giant pie and bowl of cream he'd been carrying. He walked across the room, the babies resuming their crying.

I handed my pie and ice cream off to Jemma, plucking one of the babies from Rune. The tiny human snuggled into my shoulder, crying pitifully as I rubbed soft circles across its little back.

Erik cleared his throat, handing over the letter to Gunnar. "It... it seems that someone has bequeathed their children to me."

I bounced, gratified when the baby began to quiet.

"Who?" Sune demanded. "Who did this?"

"It doesn't say," Gunnar answered for his brother, reading the note. "Just says she saw Erik on the news following last year's cruise ship rescue. When she saw Erik was in town, she decided it was a sign and left them for him. Says she won't be back for her boys."

"Dear lord," I breathed, holding the little baby closer.

"I'm sorry to do this to you, Erik. Particularly on Christmas," the Sheriff said, looking mighty uncomfortable. "I can take them home with me, or we can call Child Services. Will need to do that anyway. But I figured...what with you being named... are you the father?"

All eyes turned to Erik. His mouth flopped open, gasping like a fish.

"Oh, Erik...." Jemma sounded heartbroken. "Are you?"

"I...." He paused, frowning. "Actually, I can't be. I haven't been in a relationship since... she-who-must-not-be-named. And that was nearly two years ago."

We processed this admission, the gravity of the situation become clear. The baby in my arms couldn't have been older than a month, far too young to be left alone in the world.

"So, what do we do now?" Astrid asked, the other baby cradled in her arms.

Erik blinked, looking from one baby to another. "I guess we try to find their mother."

"And if that falls through?"

We watched Erik consider his options. With a long sigh, he rubbed a hand over his face.

"I'll seek an adoption."

Pandemonium broke out once again, Sheriff Tristan trying to bring about calm as Jemma and Sune lost their minds. Astrid handed the baby to Gunnar as she tried to referee what appeared to be the start of a long argument.

Reading the room, Rune and Liv went to the bar for another drink, while Gunnar, baby cradled against his big chest, came to me.

"This is not how I expected tonight to go," he told me, hand resting on the little baby's back.

My ovaries exploded, even as I tried to remain serious. "I doubt anyone could have predicted this."

He shook his head. "How he's gonna cope with two babies by himself is beyond me."

"We'll help him."

Gunnar looked down at me, his gaze warming. "Thanks, Valkyrie." He watched me shift the baby, settling the small bundle into a slightly more comfortable position. "That looks good on you."

"What?" I asked, bouncing slightly as the baby fussed.

"A baby. Motherhood."

I looked up at him, feeling that familiar glow light inside me. "Soon, I hope. After the wedding."

He winked. "We'll see." He looked back over at the commotion, his face tightening.

"Hey," I called, wanting to lessen his burden. "I love you."

He bent down, pressing a sweet kiss to my lips. "Love you too, baby."

I tilted my head, offering him a cheeky grin. "Besides, I know you're just jealous Erik's now beat you to the mark."

Gunnar frowned, raising an eyebrow in question.

"First grandkids." I tapped a finger lightly against the baby's back. "You can't always be first at everything, Gunnar."

He chuckled. "I'm pretty sure I always make you come first, wife-to-be."

Yeah, you do.

EPILOGUE TWO

Gunnar

Sometime in the near future...

"We're not calling our baby Cnut."
I didn't look up from the instruction manual I was attempting to decipher.

Is that a screw? Or a nail? Or some kind of hook?

"I'm serious, Gunnar. I'm not calling our child a name that could be misspelled as you-know-what," Ella hissed, hands on her hips as she leaned in, face flushed.

I tilted the manual to one side, squinting. "Do you think this was printed wrong? I can build a boat with my eyes closed but apparently can't construct a damned pram."

"Gunnar!"

I sighed, tossing the manual and getting to my feet. I pulled my fierce woman into my arms, rubbing her back.

"It was only an idea," I assured her.

"A terrible one," she told my chest, her voice slightly muffled.

I tried not to grin. "What's your choice?"

"I don't know!" She looked up, her face flushed, eyes glassy with tears. "And what if I choose horribly? What if our baby ends up with a horrible name for the rest of their life? What kind of parent will I be if—"

"Valkyrie, stop," I ordered, giving her a little squeeze. "You're going to make a wonderful mother." I reached down, placing a hand on her belly. "Our little one is going to be the luckiest kid in the world."

"Promise?"

I pressed a kiss to her forehead. "Promise."

"Good," she lifted her head, giving me a still teary blink. "Cause my water broke."

I froze. "What?"

"Yeah, my underwear is a mess. I think we should probably start getting ready to go to the hos—"

I swept her up, holding her gently as I moved us frantically through the house.

"Shit, where's your bag? Fuck. Should I call an ambulance? How close are the transactions? Jesus!"

I froze in the middle of our lounge, uncertain as to the best course of action.

"Gunnar. Gunnar, look at me."

My gaze dropped to the goddess in my arms. She raised a hand cupping my jaw. "My contractions—not transactions—are weak and far apart."

"Shit, contractions, yep. Fuck."

She ran what I assumed was meant to be a soothing hand over my cheek. "We have hours. Put me down. We'll relax, we'll time them, we'll go for a little walk to the beach, and when it's time, we'll go to the hospital. *Calmly.*" She smiled softly. "Okay?"

"Over my dead body I'm delivering our baby here," I told her. "I'm not qualified for that. I don't even know what a contraction is called!"

She laughed, sending her long hair dragging across my skin. Strangely, that small movement reassured me more than anything she could say.

I gently placed her on the floor, hands steadying her, loathed to let go.

"So this is it?" I asked, my knuckles grazing her cheek.

"Our last few hours of just us," she whispered, her smile watery.

"I'm ready, Ella. I'm so ready for this, even if it's terrifying."

"Same."

"I fucking love you, Valkyrie."

"And I fucking love you, Viking."

We grinned at each other, still as in sync today as we'd been five years ago when we'd met on that stormy night.

We spent the next few hours walking, breathing, and talking. As her contractions intensified, we headed to the hospital.

"MOTHERFUDGER!" Ella screamed, her contractions less than ten seconds apart. The baby was coming and coming fast.

"You got this, Ella," I encouraged, ignoring her crushing my hand. "Just another push. One more."

"I can't," she panted, her voice breaking. "I can't, Gunnar. I can't."

"You can." I brushed her hair away from her face, watching a new contraction rip through her body. "You're amazing, you're wonderful, you're a miracle. You're a goddess. You're a Valkyrie. You can do this, Ella. I love you."

"Nearly there," the midwife encouraged. "One more push, momma."

With a grunting groan, Ella pushed our baby into the world.

Before I could breathe, there was a flurry of movement, crying and congratulations from the hospital staff then the midwife placed a scrawling, red, bloody baby on Ella's chest.

"Congratulations!" The midwife beamed. "You've got a gorgeous little girl."

I blinked, looking down at my daughter unable to believe that this ugly, beautiful, perfect, crying, angry baby was ours.

"Freyja," Ella said, looking up at me, tears streaming down her face, her smile blinding. "Our little Freyja."

I cupped Freyja's head, pressing a fervent kiss to Ella's mouth. "Perfect."

Want more Evie Mitchell books?
Check out my website at
EvieMitchell.com

Enter the code **EBOOK10** you can get 10% off your purchase from my website.

Be sure to also sign up for my newsletter for more discounts, sneak peeks, and bookish news.

ABOUT THE AUTHOR

Hey, I'm Evie Mitchell.
I'm a thirty-something romance author
(she/her/hers) living with disability. I believe in
inclusion, accessibility, and fierce romance. My
loves include steamy romance novels, my sexy
husband, our THREE sausage dogs (THE
FUR!!!), and my ever-growing collection of
book-related mugs.

As a woman with a diverse work history,
including in areas such as hospitality, retail,
emergency response, event management,
human rights, disability access, and security—
my books are filled with true stories
(bridezillas), worst-case scenarios
(malfunctioning zippers), and my favorite
tropes (one-bed).

I'm a strong proponent of #OwnVoices, and
specialize in fiercely inclusive happily ever
afters.

EvieMitchell.com
Socials: @EvieMitchellAuthor

ALSO BY EVIE MITCHELL

All Access Series

Knot My Type

Love Flushed

Darn Knit All

Larsson Siblings

Clean Sweep

The X-List

Reality Check

The Christmas Contract

The A-List

Capricorn Cove

The Shake-up

Double the D

Muffin Top

The Mrs. Clause

New Year, Knew You

Double Breasted

As You Wish

You Sleigh Me
Meat Load
Resolution Revolution

Dogg Pack
Puppy Love
Bad English
The Frock Up
Pier Pressure
Trick or Trent
New Year's Faye

Reigning Hearts
The Marriage Claim
Silent Knight

Men of Trinity Bay
Kink in the Road

Nameless Souls MC
Runner
Wrath
Ghost
Shield

Elliot Security

Rough Edge
Bleeding Edge